The GHOSTS
of GLENCOE

The GHOSTS *of* GLENCOE

Mollie Hunter

CANONGATE KELPIES

to Michael, with love

First published 1966 by Evans Brothers Ltd
First published in Kelpies 1994

Copyright © Maureen Mollie Hunter McIlwraith 1966
Cover illustration by Alexa Rutherford

British Library Cataloguing-in-Publication Data
A catalogue record for this book is available
on request from the British Library.

ISBN 0 86241 467 9

Printed and bound in Denmark by Nørhaven A/S

CANONGATE PRESS LTD, 14 FREDERICK STREET,
EDINBURGH EH2 2HB

Contents

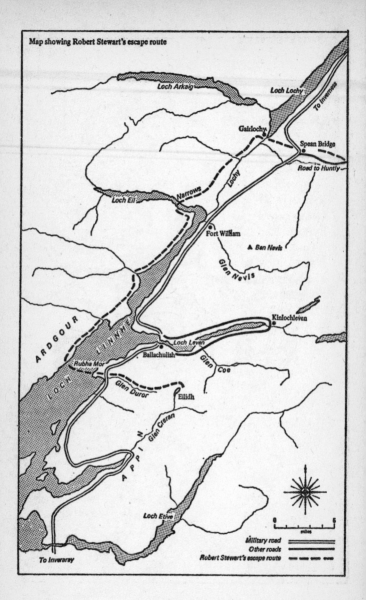

Map showing Robert Stewart's escape route

Loch Arkaig

Loch Lochy

To Inverness

Gairlochy

Spean Bridge

Road to Huntly

Lochy

Narrows

Loch Eil

Fort William

▲ Ban Nevis

Glen Nevis

ARDGOUR

Kinlochleven

LOCH LINNHE

Loch Leven

Rubha Mor

Ballachulish

Glen Coe

Glen Duror

Eilidh

APPIN

Glen Creran

Loch Etive

To Inveraray

0   5
         miles

- - - - - - Military road
_____ Other roads
– · – · – · – Robert Stewart's escape route

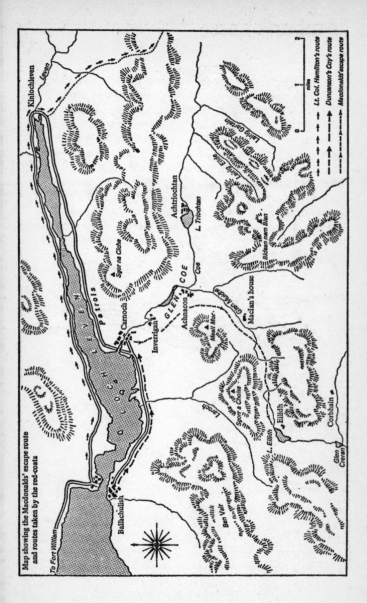

Map showing the Macdonalds' escape route and routes taken by the red-coats

Lt. Col. Hamilton's route
Duncanson's Coy's route
Macdonald's escape route

miles
0   1   2

To Fort William

Kinlochleven

Leven

Ballachulish

Carnoch

Invercoe

Achnacon

Meall Mor

Maclan's house

GLEN COE

Coe

Achtriochtan

L. Triochtan

Aonach Dubh

Glen Muidhe

Bidean nam Bian

Larach Garbh

Spor na Ciche

Patrols

LEVEN

Loch

Ben Vair

Spor a' Choire

L. Eilidh

Eilidh

Corbhain

Glen Creran

Author's note

The character of Ensign Robert Stewart in this book is based on a story current for many years among the survivors of the Massacre of Glencoe and their descendants, and the book itself sticks closely to the actual facts of the Massacre. For facilities of research into the historical background of this notorious event I am greatly indebted to Miss Anne Drysdale, Curator of the West Highland Museum, Fort William: also to Major H. Barker, MBE, of RHQ, Queen's Own Highlanders, for his assistance in my research into military matters. To my husband, for his constant encouragement in the writing of this book and for much sound advice and practical help in exploring and mapping the terrain of the story, my debt is greater than can be adequately acknowledged.

1 Highland garrison

There was a high wind sweeping the ramparts of Fort William on that night of 29th December when I was officer of the watch at the Spur Gate entrance to the Fort. It was the first truly strong gale of that winter of 1691, and so loudly did it howl around the guard-house where I sat writing my hourly report that the noise of it cut me off from all sound at the Spur Gate itself.

I did not hear the sentry crying *'Qui vive?'*, therefore, and neither did I hear the clash of sword against bayonet which followed on his challenge. My first knowledge of the trouble at the gate came when the door of the officers' duty-room was burst rudely open and the figure of a man appeared on the threshold – a figure of such fantastic appearance as to make me rise in amazement from my desk.

The man was tall – immensely so, and massively built in proportion to his height. He stood over the six and a half foot mark, and the Highland Chief's insignia of three eagle feathers flaring from his bonnet made him seem even taller. A doublet of bull's hide studded with silver encased his great chest. Tall boots of untanned leather and tight-fitting trews of red Macdonald tartan clothed his lower half. From a silver brooch on one shoulder hung a scarf of the same red tartan, and topping all this was a face as craggy and weathered as ancient rock with long grey moustachios drooping down on either side of a grim mouth and a grey forked beard jutting from his chin.

He was in his sixties, I judged – a man old enough to be my grandfather. Yet the dark eyes glaring at me above a hawk's beak of a nose were as fierce as those of any young warrior, and as those fierce eyes met mine he brought one huge hand smacking down on the hilt of the broadsword swinging at his hip.

'Is it yourself,' he roared, 'that told the sentry fellow to bar me from entering the Fort?'

The white and frightened face of the sentry appeared suddenly at his shoulder.

'I challenged him, Mr Stewart, sir,' he gasped, 'and I would have shot also when he failed to answer, but—'

'But you were not sufficiently awake to your duty,' I berated him curtly. 'Return to your post, Private MacEachern. You will be on charge for this.'

Quick, for fear of my further anger, the sentry withdrew and I faced the big man with an assurance I did not feel.

'Pray contain yourself, sir, when you address an officer of the King. The sentry has standing orders not to admit anyone who cannot reply to his *qui vive* with the correct password.'

'So?' He muttered suspicions into his beard, eyeing me the while with wariness beginning to replace his anger.

'There was no insult intended to my rank, then?' he asked eventually.

'You have my word, sir,' I told him, my heart in my mouth lest my life finish there and then at the early age of sixteen from a stroke of that broadsword of his – for there is no one more tender of his dignity than a Highland Chief, and this big fellow seemed a prime example of the touchiness of the breed.

'Then,' his hand moved reluctantly away from the hilt of his sword, 'you can be having the honour to announce me to the Governor of the Fort.'

'If you will give me your name, sir?' I suggested.

He stared hard at me. 'You are surely little acquaint with the Highlands, lad, if you have no eyes for MacIan, the Chief of the Macdonalds of Glencoe.'

'Your pardon, sir. Your rank is evident, of course, but your person *is* unknown to me. I will escort you to Colonel Hill immediately.'

He turned away from me booming, 'I have my own escort, lad – a Chief's escort,' but I stepped quickly between him and the door.

'Sir, without me you will be challenged by picquets at every other step, and since you do not have the password . . .'

Reluctantly then he yielded best to me. We stepped outside the guard-house and as we emerged I saw the pony he had ridden into the Fort. It was held by one of a group of young clansmen, their brawny legs and arms bare to the biting wind and broadswords held in readiness for whatever danger might perchance their Chief.

MacIan ordered the gillies – as these retainers of his were called – to wait at the guard-house for him, and we set off towards the Governor's Residence on the far side of the parade-ground. As we walked with our heads down against the wind, the first flurry of the snow that had been threatening for hours came swirling round our ears, and I wondered to myself what business MacIan had with the Colonel so urgent as to bring him all the way from Glencoe on a bitter December night such as this. Moreover, I thought, the New Year of 1692 was only forty-eight hours away and men did not normally travel far from home in Scotland at such a season of celebration.

Colonel Hill was not yet in bed although it was gone midnight. I saw the light in his first-floor study window and quickly took MacIan up to him. The Colonel rose to meet the old man, smiling and exclaiming with pleasure at the visit, for in his task of dealing with the troubled military situation in the Highlands it was his policy to keep on friendly terms with as many of the clan Chiefs as possible. Besides which – or so I had heard – MacIan was an old friend of his.

I hurried back to the Spur Gate guard-house, debating to myself whether or not to carry out my threat of putting Private MacEachern on a charge. After all, if he *had* fired and killed or even winged MacIan, it might have been sufficient to spark off yet another clan revolt against the Government! Moreover, MacIan was a Chief of Clan Donald. Those of the MacEachern name formed a minor branch of the same clan, and MacIan had certainly used his authority as a Chief to force his way past the sentry. Considering this aspect of the case I thought of the extreme respect in which an ordinary Highlander holds a Clan Chief and decided finally to summon MacEachern and read him a lecture instead of charging him with an offence that would certainly merit a flogging.

I had found him a good enough soldier in the ordinary way, I thought as I delivered my lecture to him, and in truth, I could not see that a flogging now would make him a better one if a similar set of circumstances were to come his way. Yet he needed to have a quicker mind for the event, and so I told him.

'You should have fired into the air, MacEachern,' I warned, 'and then presented your bayonet at the charge. That would have given time for the guard to bar entry to MacIan until I could be summoned to deal with him.'

'I – I am not on a charge then, sir? You will not have me flogged?' MacEachern stammered.

'No, this time I will not have you flogged,' I told him, '—provided you are sufficiently warned for the future!'

He gaped at me, his eyes swimming with gratitude, and as I dismissed him I wondered to myself if he was not a bit simple in the head. Certainly I had heard it told of him in the Mess that he had 'the second-sight', as Highlanders call the ability to see into the future, and I remembered saying at the time that I had no patience with men who saw visions when their minds should be attentive to their military duties.

I settled down to the rest of my spell on watch, and at three o'clock that morning as I was making my rounds of the sentries I passed MacIan out through the Spur Gate again.

The wind had risen still further by that time and the snow was whirling thickly in the darkness. I gripped the rein of MacIan's sheltie and shouted up to him through the howl of the wind.

'How far do you travel, sir?'

'To Inveraray,' he shouted back, and moved off with his gillies into the teeth of the storm.

I had had the opportunity by that time to think what his visit to the Fort might mean. MacIan's answer then told me I had suspicioned correctly and it was with foreboding in my heart that I watched his little troop disappear.

Inveraray lies more than sixty miles away along a winding track that hugs the jagged western coastline of Scotland for part of its length then plunges inland through steep mountain passes. The blizzard now blowing would be cutting cruelly across the exposed coastal section of the track and blocking the mountain passes with the snow it carried and so, if I was

12

right in my surmise, MacIan of Glencoe was in dire trouble that wild December night.

I heard none of the rumours about MacIan's visit which swept around the Fort during the following day, for my free time was spent mainly in sleeping. When I went over to the Mess that evening, however, I found myself in the thick of the matter. Most of the officers of Hill's and Argyll's, the two regiments on garrison duty in the Fort, were already in the Mess. Colonel Hill himself arrived a few moments after I did and proceeded to address the assembled officers.

The lateness of his bedding the previous night had evidently tired him and he looked all of his years as he took his place at the head of the table. The eyes in his lined, elderly face were shrewd, however, as he looked around us and began:

'Gentlemen, the senior officers here are well aware of the situation regarding MacIan, Chief of the Glencoe Macdonalds, but for the benefit of the junior officers I must explain it fully before I tell you what transpired about him last night.'

His eyes travelled down the table to where I sat with the rest of the Ensigns, and he went on:

'MacIan was one of the Chiefs who mustered his clan in 1688 on the side of the deposed Stuart King, James the Second, during the struggle between him and our present King, William the Third. Our task here at the Fort since then has been to keep the peace in the Highlands and to prevent the clans defeated in that struggle from rising again. For this purpose, the Government has demanded an oath of allegiance to King William from all the Chiefs concerned in the former fighting, and the time-limit for taking that oath expires twenty-four hours from now, on 1st January, 1692.'

'Last night—' he paused and looked directly at me, 'Ensign Robert Stewart of Argyll's Regiment admitted MacIan to the Fort and brought him to see me. He had come to swear the oath of allegiance, but as you know – and as he apparently did *not* know – the oath must be sworn before a civil authority, and I had therefore no power to administer it to him. Accordingly, I had no alternative but to send him on to the nearest Sheriff Officer at Inveraray.'

He paused again, but no one offered any immediate comment and it was clear that all those present were thinking as I had done myself the previous night. MacIan, for all his heroic stature, was still an old man and in the weather prevailing he would need great good luck to reach Inverary before the time-limit for swearing the oath. The silence lasted until Lieutenant Francis Farquhar of Hill's Regiment asked the question that was in everyone's mind.

'The oath was to be sworn on penalty of life and lands, sir. Will we be called on to take action against MacIan and his clan if he fails to swear within the time-limit?'

The Colonel sighed. 'I hope not, Farquhar. I hope not! I gave him a safe-conduct to Inverary and a letter to the Sheriff there to explain that, even if he arrived late, his intentions were good and that he should be taken into the King's mercy.'

I looked round the faces at the table to note who was in agreement with this, and saw that some officers in Argyll's wore mutinous expressions. But that was to be expected, I thought. The Macdonalds were the traditional clan-enemies of the Campbells, and Argyll's was manned and officered mainly by men of Campbell blood. Myself and the simpleton Private MacEachern were two of the few exceptions to this rule.

Major Robert Duncanson of Argyll's Regiment broke the silence.

'Sir, you are too easy with these rebel Macdonalds! Wipe out Clan Donald – exterminate the whole nest of robbers I say! *That* should be our policy!'

The Colonel's lined face flushed slightly at this and his voice had a hint of steel in it as he replied:

'It is not for soldiers to make policy, Major Duncanson. Our task is to keep the peace. Moreover, if it is war you want, you will have your fill of that soon enough.'

He nodded to Lieutenant Colonel Hamilton, the Deputy Governor of the Fort, who was sitting on his right. Hamilton opened the dispatch lying on the table in front of him and in his usual cold, precise voice he said:

'News, gentlemen. The flying packet has this day brought news from London about the campaign King William is waging against the French in Flanders.'

A murmur of excitement, quickly quelled as Hamilton went on speaking, ran round the table.

'More troops of the line are needed – urgently needed,' Hamilton said, 'and the men garrisoning this Fort form the only two reserve regiments of the strength necessary to reinforce the line. Therefore, gentlemen, the word is that we are to be drafted to the Low Countries in the spring of the New Year.'

With difficulty I restrained myself from uttering a shout of joy for this was the turn of events I had waited eagerly throughout the year I had held my commission. In the hubbub of voices that followed Hamilton's announcement I called across the table to Francis Farquhar:

'Here's an end to petty skirmishing on Outpost Patrol – eh, Francis? We shall see full field action now!'

Grinning, he called back, 'Aye – and the chance of promotion under fire to those brave enough to snatch it! You will rise to Major maybe, before you are my age, Robert!'

I laughed with him, treating it as the jest he intended it to be, but my laugh was all on the surface for I had never had any other ambition than to be a soldier. Indeed, military science was the ruling interest of my life – and how better to study this than in a full-scale campaign by King William, the greatest soldier of our day!

The Colonel quietened the hubbub with a raised hand, 'Gentlemen, Major Forbes has something to say now.'

I looked, as everyone else did, at Major Forbes, and was surprised to see an angry expression on his handsome features. Speaking stiffly, as if the words were distasteful to him, he said:

'The Colonel wishes me to speak about our training programme. As you know, our men are versed only in Highland warfare – that is, a quick firing of pistol or musket which is then thrown aside for the charge with targe and broadsword. However, the action we will meet in Flanders will call for a different military mode. It will, in fact, require rapid and sustained musket-fire followed by present bayonets from troops trained to stand their ground against a cavalry charge.'

I glanced at Francis. This was exciting news and good mili-

15

tary tactics withal. Why then should such an accomplished soldier as Forbes sound so disapproving? Francis shrugged in answer to my look, but the next words from Forbes explained the puzzle.

'I have just returned from a visit to our Commander-in-Chief at Headquarters, as you know,' he went on. 'A new training programme for the troops due for Flanders was the matter under discussion during this visit, and I must tell you now of the C-in-C's decision to send a Training Sergeant north to exercise the men of Hill's and Argyll's in these new tactics. The man's name is Sergeant Barbour, and I must also tell you now that I do not like either the man or his methods.'

'Major Forbes, you are rash. We cannot discuss that aspect of the appointment,' the Colonel said quietly. 'all we are concerned with is the man's military worth.'

My Company Commander, Captain Robert Campbell of Glenlyon asked, 'How would you rate that, Major Forbes?'

'He has an outstanding record both as a training sergeant and on the field,' Forbes admitted reluctantly, '—but I have seen him at work, Glenlyon, and believe me he is brutality incarnate!'

'The Army is not a nursery – we need men like Barbour to take the raw edges off troops like ours!'

Glenlyon laughed as he spoke and drained down the wine-glass he was holding. It was the fourth he had drunk since I entered the Mess and I realized that, as usual at this time of day, he was a little tipsy. There was a flush on the cheekbones of his long, narrow face, and the greyish-fair hair falling to his shoulders was somewhat disarranged. The Colonel looked pointedly at him as he reached for the decanter again, but it was Lieutenant Colonel Hamilton who spoke.

'Gentlemen, we cannot quarrel with the Commander-in-Chief's decision or with Headquarters policy – and I, for one, am in favour of it.'

'Boot-licker!' I thought to myself, but quickly pushed the thought away again, telling myself that I had no right to judge the situation simply on the yardstick of my liking for Forbes and my dislike of Hamilton.

'There is one point you must continue to bear in mind,

however,' the Colonel followed Hamilton's remark, 'and that is – no matter how dire the need for Hill's and Argyll's in the Flanders campaign, we still cannot be spared from the Reserve until it is certain that peace is secured in the Highlands. For King William cannot afford the risk of the Highland Chiefs rising again in favour of James the Second while all his forces are committed abroad.'

'Sir,' Major Forbes asked, 'how many rebel Chiefs have still to take the oath now, apart from MacIan of Glencoe? I recall that before I left for Edinburgh there had still been no submission from either Macdonell of Glengarry or Macdonald of Keppoch.'

'Keppoch took the oath a week ago,' the Colonel told him, 'but Glengarry has totally refused to do so. He has retired to his castle and is defying the Government from there, and so we shall doubtless hear soon from Headquarters that we must march out against him.'

Forbes nodded. 'Aye, sir, Glengarry will have to pay the price of defiance. Yet if the Glencoe Macdonalds are willing to swear loyalty, 'twould be pity if we had to march against them also. We must hope old MacIan reaches Inveraray in time.'

With a sudden malice that surprised me, Lieutenant Colonel Hamilton said, 'That he will not if Captain Drummond meets up with him at Balcardine!'

There was a little ripple of laughter at this from some of the Campbell officers for Captain Drummond was presently on Outpost Duty commanding the detachment of Argyll's that formed the garrison of Balcardine Castle on the road to Inveraray; he was a Lowland Scot and was known to have a fierce hatred of all Highland rebels.

'Gentlemen!' the Colonel said sharply. The ripple of laughter died away. Eyes were cast down and once again the mutinous look appeared on the faces of some of the officers in Argyll's. With a dignified formality that was crushing in its effect the Colonel said to Hamilton:

'Sir, you appear to have forgotten that I, personally, guaranteed MacIan safe-conduct to Inveraray.'

Hamilton's pale face flushed an ugly red at the rebuke. His

17

thin features pinched even tighter with suppressed anger, he folded the dispatch again, but Colonel Hill was a diplomat as well as a Military Governor and he knew how to restore good humour. Rising to his feet he commanded,

'Fill your glasses and be upstanding, gentlemen. I have a toast to propose.'

We stood, raising full glasses, and lifting his own glass high the Colonel cried, 'Gentlemen, to peace in the Highlands – and to war in Flanders.'

'Peace in the Highlands! War in Flanders!' we shouted in unison. And if some pledged the one more heartily than the other the fact went unnoticed in the massed sound of our voices.

We drank, and for my part I confess that I never drank a toast with more relish in my life!

A week later, Sergeant Barbour arrived at the Fort. I was still on night-duty but nevertheless I was required to attend his first demonstration of the new musket that was being issued to the troops. This was for the benefit of officers only, and to begin with most of us were too taken up in examining the musket itself to pay much attention to the Sergeant himself.

The Army in England already had this musket and, so we had heard, the men there had nicknamed it affectionately, 'Brown Bess'; the 'brown' being from its colour and 'bess' being their own corruption of the Dutch word 'bus' for a gun, for it had been in use in Holland before our Government decided to take it up.

I measured one and found it was forty-two inches over-all, a fine weapon indeed, beautifully balanced and sighted, and the new snap-haunce trigger action a vast improvement on the old matchlock. The bayonet slid smoothly and cleanly out from its sheath beneath the barrel, and clipped on to the muzzle with one quick, neat action. Major Forbes came up to me as I was sighting along the barrel and delighting in the feel of the smoothly-turned butt against my cheek. His hand fell heavily on my shoulder and he smiled at the expression of pleasure on my face.

'Well, Stewart, 'twill be easy to put the Frenchies on the run with a weapon like that!'

Before I could answer, Lieutenant Colonel Hamilton called for silence so that Sergeant Barbour could address us. The Sergeant stepped forward and we all turned to look curiously at him.

He was a short, stockily-built man of about forty-five years with a head as round as a cannon-ball, harsh craggy features, and close-clipped iron-grey hair. His eyes were the same colour as his hair and so deep-set that they seemed only a dark glint behind the bony ridge of his cheek-bones. His speech had the broad vowels and strong rolling r's of the Lowland Scot and because of this I had some difficulty in following him at first, for, what with a French mother and an up-bringing in Holland where my father had been an officer in the Scots Brigade, I was more accustomed to French speech than to English.

The Gaelic-speaking officers among us, to whom English was also a second language, were likewise puzzled by Barbour's uncouth Lowland dialect. The action of the musket itself, however, was so clear and simple that it solved the worst of the problem for us, and by the time Barbour reached his exposition of the new drill tactics we had found greater ease in following him.

Rendered as nearly as possible into fair English, his speech to us was on these lines. He began by telling us that a continuous barrage of musket-fire from alternating front and rear ranks would be our aim for infantry formations from that time forward.

'And this, gentlemen,' he explained, 'will be achieved by a drill pattern that provides for loading by one rank while the other one fires. Thus, initial fire by front rank will be followed by advance of rear rank into former front rank positions. Rear rank therefore advances, presents and fires while front rank recovers and re-loads. The pattern is then reversed to initial positions, and this alternating of front and rear ranks into firing positions continues indefinitely to give sustained musket-fire as long as required Bayonets will be fixed throughout and a triple bayonet-thrust incorporated into the drill so

19

that the front rank is at no time overwhelmed by a charge on the part of the enemy and the sudden necessity thereby for fighting at close quarters.'

I nudged Francis Farquhar and looked at him with raised eyebrows. Argyll's had been in existence for only two years and the ranks were composed of men who knew little more than how to swing a broadsword. How difficult was it going to be for them to master the intricacies of this complicated drill?

Francis only grinned in reply to my worried look. As well he might, I thought enviously. Hill's had been formed from two veteran regiments, now disbanded. The ranks were filled by experienced men who had seen many changes of tactics in their time and so they would doubtless be able to take this one also in their stride.

'It will all be done to numbers,' Francis whispered reassuringly. ' 'Twill only be a matter of time before they grasp it.'

But time, I quickly realized, was not only the only matter to be taken into account in the practice of the new drill. There was also Sergeant Barbour's vaunting pride in himself as an instructor to reckon with. That, and his brutal disregard for the fact that men have a breaking-point beyond which they can endure no more fatigue or pain.

The parades for musket-instruction were endless for the Sergeant was content with nothing short of absolute accuracy in the drill. The men's feet swelled with the long hours of standing in the parade-ground. Their hands became chapped in the bitter weather that prevailed so that the skin of their fingers broke and bled when they worked the cocking-piece and trigger of their muskets. There were several cases of frostbite, and what with the fatigue of these parades and poor feeding due to the running-down of our winter supplies, there was a greater degree of sickness than usual in the ranks.

'There *is* a purpose in Barbour's methods, according to Hamilton,' Francis Farquhar told me one day when I was inveighing against the Sergeant. 'If this drill is to serve its purpose truly, it seems, the men must be so perfect in it that they can carry it out anytime, anywhere. Let a man be dead drunk, wounded, or paralysed with fear, Hamilton says, and provided the drill has been sufficiently drummed into him he will still carrry it out on the battle-field exactly as he did on the parade-ground.'

And so Sergeant Barbour's bullying continued unchecked and each day he continued to preface his instructions to the troops with the cry:

'Now hear this, my bully boys! You will march forth from here as soldiers fit to fight for the King, or else be carried forth in your shrouds. This I swear for you!'

That was his constant boast to them, and to us. And as bad luck would have it for the men, it was Lieutenant Colonel Hamilton who was in charge of punishment parades that January, Colonel Hill being laid a-bed with another attack of the rheumatism that troubled him. Men were put on charge for allowing a spot of damp to appear in the priming-pans of their muskets, for being too slow on the 'fix bayonets' order, for not dressing the firing-line properly. Lieutenant Colonel Hamilton handed down the severe sentences that the Sergeant urged, and the flogging triangle was in daily use.

Even the disciplinarians among the officers began to mutter restively, and one evening Major Forbes exploded to Hamilton in the Mess.

'He is pushing the men too far and too fast, sir! There is no fighting for months ahead yet!'

'Indeed, Major?' Hamilton smiled the thin smile that was all he ever permitted himself. ' 'Tis scarcely wise, is it, to forecast what fighting there might be for a regiment on active service unless you are in possession of *all* the facts of the political situations.'

He walked away leaving Forbes staring after him with a bewildered look that changed quickly to one of angry suspicion before he, too, stalked out of the Mess. None of the other officers in the Mess at the time speculated on what Hamilton's remark might mean, and I had the uneasy feeling that this was not because there were present those, like myself, who were very junior in rank. I recalled the smile, quickly concealed, which had crossed Glenlyon's face while Hamilton spoke, and I wondered if the lack of discussion now could be due to the fact that some of the officers there already knew the meaning of Hamilton's words. Yet Forbes was senior to them all. Why should he be kept in ignorance of something known to Glenlyon and the other officers?

'There is some mystery here that needs ferreting out,' Francis Farquhar said to me later when we discussed the incident. I did not trouble myself unduly over what that mystery might be, however, for my spell of night-guard was ended; I had a few days leave due to me as a result of it, and I intended to spend that leave on a visit home.

2 Secret dispatches

I called it 'home', but in truth, I had no real home for my life until a year past had been spent in travelling with my parents wherever my father had been posted with the Scots Brigade. Then, in my fifteenth year, my father was killed on service with his regiment. My mother's wish had been to return to her own home in France then, but first she had thought it her duty to bring me on a visit to my father's people in Appin, some eighteen miles distant from Fort William in the northwest Highlands of Scotland.

Less than a month after we arrived in Glen Creran in Appin, however, she herself had died of a flux. I had stayed on in Glen Creran at the command of my Great-Aunt Euphemia, the head of my father's family of the Stewarts of Eilidh in Glen Creran, dividing my time between her home and that of my Uncle Ian and Aunt Fiona at Corbhain, a mile distant from Eilidh. Of these two households I much preferred Corbhain, since there I was both free of Great-Aunt Euphemia's forbidding presence and had my cousin Elizabeth for company, and so it was in my Aunt Fiona's house that I meant to spend my leave once I had satisfied duty by paying my New Year respects at Eilidh.

I had five days in hand, from the 27th to the 31st of January, and when the weather turned suddenly milder on the morning of the 27th I foresaw some pleasant days hunting in my uncle's company. I went over the smithy, where my horse was being shod, in a high good humour and very eager to be off.

My mount, a young grey I had named Shadow after the grey which had carried my father into so many campaigns, was ready and waiting for me. I had my father's brass-bound flint-lock pistol thrust into my belt, his basket-hilted sword swung by my side, and as I mounted Shadow and urged him forward I could almost feel on my shoulders the heavy gold of the Lieutenant Colonel's epaulettes my father had once worn.

I would win them in Flanders, I thought cheerfully – or at least, I would make the Flanders campaign my first step towards winning them!

I had only one more thing do do before I left the Fort and that was to collect a letter from Francis Farquhar for my cousin Elizabeth. There was an understanding between the two of them and Francis was only waiting for his promotion to Captain before he proposed marriage. Meanwhile, I was the courier for their letters and got much amusement out of teasing Elizabeth to blushes whenever I carried one from Francis home to her.

I trotted Shadow off across the parade-ground, and as it happened, met Francis half-way in the company of Gilbert Kennedy, his fellow Lieutenant in Hamilton's Company. Gilbert was Dispatch Officer on that month's duty-list. His hands were full of papers and he and Francis had their heads together deep in conversation as I rode up to them.

'The letter, Francis,' I called, nearing them.

He looked up with a start and produced the letter from the cuff of his uniform coat. As I tucked it into my own cuff Gilbert Kennedy took a brief farewell of us and hurried off in the direction of Lieutenant Colonel Hamilton's quarters.

'I must be off too,' I said, preparing to turn Shadow's head.

Francis caught the horse's bridle and said hurriedly, 'Wait, Robert! Gil had something very curious to say to me just now.'

'Eh? What's that?' I was truly impatient to be off and I could not imagine a quiet fellow like Gil Kennedy with anything very exciting to say.

'He spoke about Hamilton,' Francis said, 'and that odd remark he made to Forbes last night in the Mess.' He hesitated for a moment and then went on with a rush, 'Gil says that Hamilton has been corresponding for some time now with Stair, the Secretary of State for Scotland, and he says also that Hamilton has been careful to keep the correspondence secret from Colonel Hill!'

This *was* curious news – enough to make me put a sharp check on Shadow's restlessness and to protest, 'Oh, come, Francis! Gil must be mistaken! Would Hamilton dare to deceive the Colonel so – and what business could he have, in any case, with one in such high political office as Stair?'

'All men in high office have their jackals!' Francis snapped, 'and Gil is too sensible to have made a mistake over this. Hamilton *has* some scheme afoot, and he *is* deceiving the Colonel over it.'

'Then he must have good warrant for his action!' I retorted, and pulled Shadow's head sharply round towards the gate. 'Forgive me, Francis. I have not time for riddles just now. I must be away.'

He frowned in annoyance at being thus dismissed but as I moved off called anxiously, 'Do not forget the letter for Elizabeth!' I waved to show I had heard him and set Shadow to a canter out through the Spur Gate and on to the home-road for Appin.

The conversation with Francis stayed in my mind for the first mile or so of the road, and I wondered what possible affair Hamilton was involved in that had to be kept secret from the Colonel. It must be an important matter, I thought, if an official of the high importance of the Secretary of State was concerned in it also!

The morning was so fair, however, and the feeling of being on leave so pleasant, that my thoughts soon wandered off this track. Moreover, having spent nearly all my life in flat country I was still greatly taken with the wildness of the High-land scene, and I rode along with my eyes travelling from one to the other of the mountains towering all round me and mar-velling at the grandeur of their sheer, dark sides and snow-capped peaks.

This first part of my home-road lay along the military route which runs up from the south to where the Fort stands at the head of the great western sea-inlet of Loch Linnhe. From Fort William the road then bears northeastwards right through the Great Glen to the east-coast garrison at Inverness, thus com-pleting the chain of communication between the south and the garrisons at either end of the only feasible military route through the Highlands. Even while I was admiring the wild mountain country around me, therefore, I was approving the strategy which had garrisoned it so effectively, and it was on such military matters that I dwelt mainly for the rest of my two hours ride along the southern bank of Loch Linnhe.

This brought me to the point where Loch Leven joins Loch Linnhe and runs east from it, and here I turned east to ride along Loch Levenside for a mile till I reached the village of Ballachulish. I crossed Loch Leven on the ferry at Ballachulish, then bore east for another mile on Leven's southern shore, and so came to the Laroch Pass running south past Ben Vair into Glen Creran.

I was now completely off any made track. My pace therefore slowed considerably, for the path through the Laroch Pass was not only a rough one, it was still partly hidden by the snow from the great blizzard at the end of December. Shadow was nimble at all the obstacles, however, and myself being in vigorous enough health not to be affected by the effort of our scrambling progress, we still managed to reach Glen Creran just short of mid-day.

The path by the bank of Loch Eilidh was well-travelled. Shadow forged swiftly along it and on the stroke of noon I was at Eilidh. Great-Aunt Euphemia had just sat down to dinner when I came into the house, and to my surprise, my cousin Elizabeth was seated at the table with her.

'Is this a New Year visit, Elizabeth?' I asked when greetings had been exchanged and I had taken my place beside her.

Elizabeth pressed her lips firmly together and looked from me to Great-Aunt Euphemia. Without answering, she bent her head over her plate. A wing of her red-gold hair swung forward with the movement and hid her face from me and, puzzled by her silence, I looked to Great-Aunt Euphemia for enlightenment.

Her head was turned from me towards the silver salver of venison which Duncan, her major-domo, was presenting for carving. He caught the glance I directed at her and said briskly, 'She is here to learn to heed her elders and betters, Master Robert, so let you be more at your dinner and less at the questions.'

I had never become used to the familiarity shown by servants in the Highlands. Nor did I agree with their belief that, being of the same clan and therefore of one blood with their masters, they were entitled to use such familiarity of speech.

I glared haughtily at Duncan but his only response was to nudge my great-aunt and say wonderingly, 'Will ye be looking at these two bairns, mistress! They are as much the dead spit of one another as if they were brother and sister and not just first cousins! The same colour o' hair, the same Stewart features – and the same bright blue eyes glaring at ye when they are out o' temper.'

'Really, Great-Aunt,' I protested. 'Must you permit such insolence!'

Great-Aunt Euphemia surveyed me over the salver of venison. Her hair was white with the many years of her age but she, too, still had the bright blue Stewart eyes and they were sparking as angrily at me as mine were at her.

'After forty years in my service I should hope that Duncan knows his manners to me,' she snapped. 'And you, that are half-French by birth although your father was the eldest son and the heir to Eilidh, you will do well to remember that Duncan's blood is *all* Stewart and he is therefore as entitled to offer an opinion on family affairs – with my permission – as you are!'

I gritted my teeth on my anger and said as calmly as I could, 'Very well, madam. What family affair is concerned?'

'I have arranged a match for Elizabeth,' she told me haughtily, 'a highly advantageous match with a young kinsman of the Earl of Breadalbane. However your cousin insists on the prior claim of some ridiculous attachment she says she has to an officer in your regiment, and she therefore presumes to object to my efforts on her behalf. Accordingly, she is here under my hand until – as Duncan has said – she learns to heed her elders and betters.'

'But Great-Aunt, she and Francis are – that is, they have an – an understanding!' I floundered protestingly.

'Hold your tongue, Robert! An *understanding*, indeed, with a future-less young Lieutenant when I am offering her the advantages of marriage with an Earl's kinsman!'

Elizabeth's chair crashed suddenly back against the sideboard as she jumped to her feet and ran blindly out of the room.

'Elizabeth!'

There was no reply to my great-aunt's commanding call after her, and she turned back to her venison remarking angrily, 'She will have a rod laid across her back for this!'

The little appetite I had left was banished by this remark. As soon as I could courteously do so I left the table and went off to find Elizabeth. She was in her own room, standing looking silently out of the window. I gave her the letter from Francis and left her to read it in peace while I went out to the stables. I wanted the company of horses and grooms to take the taste of this women's quarrel out of my mouth, and as I walked, I cursed the misfortune that had brought me into the midst of their feminine bickering.

Yet I pitied Elizabeth, for I had an affection for her. I had shared the same dogs, the same books, the same tutor with her when I first came to Glen Creran. And unlike my grown Stewart relations who had found amusement in one so young as myself being so deeply concerned with all things military, she had been prepared to listen patiently to my endless talk of fosse and glacis, of culverin and demi-culverin, of march and counter-march.

I wondered if I should postpone visiting Aunt Fiona and Uncle Ian till my next leave. This would deprive me of the pleasure of hunting in my uncle's company, but Duncan could show me some good stalking on the mountains round Loch Eilidh and leaving Elizabeth just now seemed a somewhat callous thing to do.

It was almost like desertion in the face of the enemy, I thought, remembering how Great-Aunt Euphemia had tried to force me, too, to her will before I succeeded in entering Argyll's Regiment. She had disapproved as greatly of that as she had disapproved of my father's service in King William's Scots Brigade for, like most of the Appin Stewarts, she was an ardent supporter of the deposed James the Second. The politics of my choice mattered nothing to me, of course. It was soldiering only that had my interest, and I recalled then how I had had to threaten to join Argyll's as a private gentleman volunteer in the ranks before she finally gave her consent to my commission.

There was no such threat I could bring forward on Elizabeth's behalf, however, and so it seemed as if she had no choice but to bow to Great-Aunt Euphemia's wishes. But it would cheer her, at least, if I spent my leave at Eilidh. And she was very fond of Shadow. If I stayed at Eilidh she could ride him as often as she wished.

I made the offer to her later that day. Her face brightened for a moment, and then grew mournful again.

'What am I going to do, Rob?' she asked desperately. 'The old witch has father and mother on her side, too. She is the head of the family, they say, and so I must obey her. I would be cursed, else, and so would they.'

'Francis will think of something,' I told her uneasily. 'Perhaps he could persuade Colonel Hill to speak to Great-Aunt Euphemia – he was a great friend of hers in their younger days, I am told.'

'She has forgotten what it is like to be young!' Elizabeth cried despairingly. 'They have all forgotten, Rob!'

I decided then that I had no choice but to stay on at Eilidh. Clearly Elizabeth looked on me now as her only ally and I could not desert her. Yet I had no inclination to exchange the discipline of the Fort for my great-aunt's iron rule, and so I spent as little time in the house as possible and persuaded Elizabeth to do likewise. I kept my promise also of giving her Shadow to ride, contenting myself with a sturdy hill-garron from my great-aunt's stable, and was rewarded by Elizabeth's vast pleasure in the swift young grey whenever there was opportunity to let him have his head.

Corbhain being forbidden to her, I could not slip away for some hunting with my uncle on the pretext of carrying Elizabeth on a visit home, but on my third day at Eilidh I had a day's stalking with Duncan. We used the bows and arrows traditional in these parts for deer-hunting, and managed to bring down a stag apiece. Mine was a big beast, a twelve-pointer. My satisfaction at this and Duncan's praise of the fine kill I had made warmed me to him, and I left Eilidh at last feeling that my leave had not been entirely wasted.

I carried a letter from Elizabeth to Francis with me, but I had no opportunity to deliver it immediately for as soon as I arrived back at the Fort late on the 31st of January I was caught up in other matters.

The sentry shouted down the usual '*Qui vive?*' I shouted back the reply '*Vive le roi Guillaume!*' and followed it up with the required account of my name, rank and regiment. Satisfied, the sentry swung the gate open and as he did so another voice called from the darkness.

'Mr Stewart, sir? Be pleased to receive an urgent message in the guard-house, sir.'

I dismounted and hurried into the Spur Gate guard-house. Lieutenant Lindsay of my own Company – a taciturn young man and a relative of Glenlyon's – was in the officers' duty-room talking to the officer of the watch. He swung round as I entered and when he saw who it was, said,

'Ah, Stewart. You are back in time.'

'In time for what?'

He pushed past me to the door. 'You are to report immediately to Glenlyon's quarters. The Company is moving out at dawn tomorrow.'

I followed him, throwing questions at his back, but outside the door I had to pause while I arranged for a groom to stable Shadow. Then I was off across the parade-ground after Lindsay. He was making for Glenlyon's quarters and reached there before I did. I followed him in and presented myself to my Company Commander.

My arrival made the full complement of officers in Glenlyon's Company, I noted, for my fellow-Ensign, Lundie, was already there. He was yet another relative of Glenlyon's – a beefy fellow about two years older than myself, and I had always thought him rather stupid. For once, however, there was an animated look on his face, and as for Glenlyon he was positively sparkling with high spirits.

'Ah, Robert m'boy,' he greeted me effusively. 'We were afraid you might not arrive back in time to share our good fortune.'

'Well, sir, I would have reported back early tomorrow morning if my leave had gone as planned, but—'

'But it did not, eh? And so you will be in time to march to Glencoe with us!'

30

'Glencoe, sir?'

'Aye, there is a great dispersal of the garrison been decided on. Quarters are too cramped in the Fort for all of us and food is running low. And so we are to be billeted out – and while we are about it, maybe collect some of the tax-money Clan Donald owes to the Government! We will drink to that, shall we?'

'Yes, sir,' I said.

I was disappointed. Billeting out of the Fort might be a pleasant enough change, but I could see no cause for celebration in that or in the prospect of levelling a musket to persuade some poverty-stricken clansman to part with the money for his taxes. I took the glass of wine Lieutenant Lindsay silently handed to me and Glenlyon laughed at my glum face.

'Come, boy, you have not heard the whisper of action yet, have you!'

I looked up from my glass with hope returning to me. Glenlyon's face was flushed, his eyes were bright, in the candlelight his hair seemed more fair than grey. Suddenly he seemed to have shed full twenty years of his age.

'Action!' he repeated, enjoying my suspense. 'The word is out, Ensign Stewart, that Macdonell of Glengarry may no longer be safe in that castle of his! The Government in London is highly displeased with his defiance in locking himself away there, and our Regiment may be taking a tilt at him soon.'

'Only may, sir? Is it not settled, then?'

' 'Tis settled enough. Settled enough to drink to,' Glenlyon said. 'We will not be long in Glencoe before the orders come through to march against Glengarry – take my word for that!'

'We will need siege tackle,' I mused, a picture of Glengarry's strongly-built castle in my mind.

'That will be seen to – Lieutenant Colonel Hamilton has all the details in hand,' Glenlyon told me. 'Now let us drink.'

He raised his glass. Lindsay, Lundie and myself followed suit, and we drank to the reduction of Castle Glengarry.

'One thing I must enjoin on you,' Glenlyon said with sudden seriousness as we lowered our glasses. 'Let no word of the action proposed against Glengarry escape you while we are in Glencoe. Remember, the Macdonalds of Glencoe and the Macdonells of Glengarry are all members of Clan Donald, and if the Glencoe men get the least wind of our intentions they will put their Glengarry cousins on the *qui vive* and so lose us the advantage of surprise. Guard your tongues, therefore, while we are in Glencoe.'

We all duly acknowledged this instruction and then, turning to me, Glenlyon added, 'Oh, and Stewart – one more thing. Sergeant Barbour is now assigned as the senior sergeant in my Company – for this expedition at least.'

I put my wine-glass down, careful not to let any expression show in my face.

'Very good, sir. With your permission now, sir, I will go and prepare for an early start tomorrow.'

Glenlyon nodded. 'Till reveille, Stewart.'

I said, 'Goodnight, sir,' nodded my farewell to the other two, and went out.

Once outside I gave vent to my feelings in a growl of disgust. Why did Hamilton have to spoil the pleasure of this expedition by attaching the detestable Barbour to Glenlyon's Company!

Still thinking of this I hurried over to the stables to inspect the work of the orderly who had taken Shadow. The grey had been rubbed down, fed and watered, and satisfied by this I went off to see Francis Farquhar and give him Elizabeth's letter before I retired for the night.

I found him lying on his bed in his own quarters. He was stretched out with his hands behind his head, one knee cocked over the other, his gaze gloomily contemplating the mud on the boot thus displayed. He rolled over when he saw me and snatched the letter eagerly from my hand, but I stopped him as he was about to break the seal on it for I had no wish to be present when he learned Elizabeth's news.

'Before you read, Francis,' I said hurriedly, 'have you heard that Glenlyon's Company is moving out tomorrow?'

He nodded. 'Aye, the expedition against Glengarry – is that what Glenlyon told you?'

'Yes, of course. There is nothing more to it, is there?'

'I wish I knew, Robert.' He drummed absently on the letter with his finger-tips and then said suddenly, 'I had a word with Major Forbes the day you went on leave, Rob. I told him what Gil Kennedy had told me that same morning, but he already knew of the letters that have been passing back and forth between Hamilton and his powerful friends.'

'So he sent you off with a flea in your ear?'

'That he did not! He as much as told me that the true power in the Fort has virtually passed from Hill into Hamilton's hands.'

'What warrant has he for thinking so?'

'This warrant,' Francis said slowly. 'You know that when he is at Headquarters in Edinburgh he has authority to open such dispatches as may arrive there from London for forwarding to Colonel Hill. Well, although he did not tell me so in so many words, I gathered from the way he spoke that he had seen enough to convince him of this in the dispatches he read and then sent on to Colonel Hill during his last stay in Edinburgh.'

I stared uneasily at him and asked, 'Could you not have pressed him to be more exact in his words, Francis?'

Francis shrugged and said irritably, 'A Lieutenant does not press a Major for information, you ninny! Any more questions from me would only have made him realize how indiscreet he had been to discuss the matter with me at all!'

He looked tired, I thought. He also had a look of great worry about him. Why was he concerning himself so much over what our senior officers did, I wondered, and why should he be confiding all his worrying to me, six years his junior. As if he guessed my thoughts, Francis looked up at me.

'You are young for me to be speaking to you like this,' he said, 'and yet for friendship's sake and because I am drawn to you through Elizabeth I feel I must talk to you about it. There is something rotten at the foot of all this, Rob. I say that because I know Hamilton and therefore I know there is no underhand trick he would not stoop to, to gain promotion. I know Forbes. He is an honourable man – so much so that he is sometimes slow to understand the workings of minds more devious than his own. I know the Colonel and a more upright man and better soldier never breathed, but he is old now and failing in health. He would be easy to stab in the back – and Hamilton is just the man to do so.'

Puzzled, I asked, 'But what concern has all this with the expedition proposed against Glengarry?'

'I told you,' Francis said irritably. 'I do not know. But I feel in my bones 'tis a cover for something else – for some under-handed device of Hamilton's planning.'

He stared at me. 'Do *you* not think so?'

I shrugged the question away. 'I cannot think it will do any good to speculate,' I told him. 'And now I must be off if I am to have any sleep at all before reveille.'

He turned to his letter again, but once more I checked him. I was unhappy for him, thinking of what lay therein, and unhappy for Elizabeth too, left alone with our formidable great-aunt. Quickly, before Francis could scan the first words of the letter, I voiced the thought which had flashed into my mind.

'Francis, Shadow will be eating his head off in the stables while I am away on this expedition and we cannot tell how long it will last. Could you send him to Elizabeth for me? She is staying at Eilidh just now, with our great-aunt. She is lonely there and has little to do, and you know how she loves riding Shadow.'

He smiled at me. ' 'Tis a kind thought. I will have the grey sent off tomorrow.'

'A good night to you, then,' I said, and left him quickly.

I felt a coward, running off so, but I had had enough of confidences for one night. Moreover, I was but little interested in regimental squabbles or matrimonial tangles. I *was* eager to reach my quarters, however, and inspect all my equipment for the start of the expedition on the following day!

34

3 The red soldiers

An hour after reveille on the following morning Glenlyon's Company set off for Glencoe by way of the military road to the south. We swung out of the Spur Gate one hundred and twenty strong – a hundred and twenty-three if the two drummers and the piper with us were to be taken into account, and our order of march was thus.

At our head marched the piper with a drummer on either side of him blowing and beating out the time of a war-rant of Clan Campbell. Solitary and tall behind these three, with the sun glinting off his steel breast-plate, hat in hand and his long hair blowing to the wind, marched Campbell of Glenlyon. Ensign Lundie and myself followed abreast. Behind us the men marched in six troops of eighteen men each with a Corporal to every troop. Lieutenant Lindsay strode behind the third troop and Sergeants Barbour and Hendrie brought up the rear.

I was merry and my spirits were high. I looked from the snows of Ben Nevis on my left glowing pink in the morning sun to the sparkling blue waters of Loch Linnhe on my right, and could have wished for no fairer morning in which to be alive and no better purpose than to be marching off into action – even this small action that was promised against Glengarry! I thought the men looked tidy, if not smart, in their grey breeches, and with the new muskets gleaming bright at the slope against their red coats they made a brave show of colour.

Once in Flanders, I thought, they would soon cease to be simply a clan-regiment wrapped up in its own petty feuds with other clans. There they would be absorbed into a great body of fighting-men with a larger purpose in mind. And thinking thus and remembering their hard training with Sergeant Barbour, I felt kindly towards the men of Glenlyon's Company.

Glynlyon shared my high spirits, it seemed. When the piper and the drummers ceased their music and fell back into the ranks, he called Lundie and myself to step even with him, and throughout the twelve miles to our first halt at Ballachulish he talked in the most entertaining way.

I had never seen him like this before for my relationship with him until then had been limited to duty matters. However, I had often noted the heartiness of the laughter from groups of officers round him in the Mess, and on the first leg of our journey that morning I discovered where the secret of his popularity lay. He talked well and wittily and the stories he told showed that he was both well-travelled and well-read. I enjoyed listening to him – although at times he struck me as being rather more frivolous than his grey hair would warrant, but Ensign Lundie was as lumpish as ever and seemed not to grasp the point of the wittier jests that were made.

'A sup of claret will liven his brain,' Glenlyon said to me, winking, when we halted at Ballachulish ferry.

He called Barbour to announce a general break for a meal, and while the men squatted to their oaten bannocks and ale he unstoppered the wine his orderly brought up to him. I found that oaten bannocks washed down with claret made an excellent meal and said so, and Glenlyon laughed heartily.

'We will feed fatter than that in Glencoe,' he promised. 'They have good winter provender there of sea-trout and venison, and old MacIan keeps a fair stock of fine French brandy.'

Spirits were not my tipple, I having promised my father not to indulge in such till I was a man grown, but from politeness I forebore to tell Glenlyon so lest I should seem to be criticizing his tendency to over-indulge in them.

We formed up again to cross the Ballachulish ferry, disembarked on the southern side of Loch Leven and turned east to march to Glencoe. So far this was the same route I had taken on my journey to Glen Creran, but instead of turning south again when we were level with the opening of the Laroch Pass we marched on past it and continued east for another three miles till we were almost in the shadow of the great sugar-loaf peak that marked the entrance to Glencoe.

' 'Tis called Sgor na Ciche,' Glenlyon told me, seeing me staring up at its soaring height.

Our Company Commander's spirits had remained high for

this latter part of the march, and even when we saw a small knot of men in Macdonald tartan approaching us from the houses clustered at the foot of Sgor na Ciche he continued to jest, calling, 'There is the welcoming party out to greet us!'

I was not so sure myself that it was a welcoming party. The approaching group was about twenty strong and had a very purposeful air about it. Glenlyon, however, continued unruffled. He brought the Company to a halt and called up Lieutenant Lindsay to join the group of officers at the head of it.

'That looks like John, MacIan's eldest son, leading the Macdonald band,' he observed. 'And if I mistake not, that is his young brother, my nephew Alasdair Og MacIan beside him.'

I looked my astonishment for I had no idea that our Campbell commander was related to Clan Donald. Glenlyon caught my look, laughed a little and admitted:

'I am stretching the relationship a little, Stewart, Alasdair's wife is a niece-by-marriage to my own wife – and that only by a former marriage of hers. Still, it does no harm to claim kinship where it can benefit!'

He grinned again, rather slyly, when he said this and I found both the implication of the words and the expression on his face distasteful. I turned away to watch the Macdonalds thinking that there were some curious aspects to my Company Commander of which I was bound to learn more now that I was to live at close quarters with him.

The group approaching us drew to within a few feet and halted, making no sign in reply to Glenlyon's hand raised in welcome. The senior of the two young men leading it called,

'What is your purpose in Glencoe, Glenlyon? Do you come in peace or war?'

'In peace – what else!' Glenlyon cried jovially. 'Would I come in war against my own kinsman?'

The two young leaders exchanged glances. They moved a step or two nearer to us, their band following, and the older one, John, asked:

'What's to do then, Glenlyon?'

'Why, my boy, 'tis this. We are turned out of the Fort!'

Glenlyon laughed, slapping his thigh at the jest, and then more seriously said, ' 'Tis a matter of necessity I fear, John. Quarters are too tight for us all to be contained in the Fort just now and our winter food-stocks are low. So the Government has chosen to billet us on you for the next week or two, and right sorry as I am that we should eat up your good winter provender, I fear it must be so.'

'You are sure you have no war-like intentions against us?' the younger brother, Alasdair, asked suspiciously.

'Against my own wife's nephew and his kin!' Glenlyon cried boisterously. 'D'ye take me for a rogue, boy? Why, 'tis Government protection, not punishment, you will have all the time we are in the glen!'

There could have been no fairer statement of intention, and though Alasdair continued to eye us suspiciously, John was clearly satisfied by it. Seeing this, Glenlyon seized the moment to present us officers to the two young men, and there were salutes and bows of introduction between us. A word from the Chief's eldest son then sent the Macdonald men loping swiftly back towards the houses. Glenlyon gave the signal for our troop to move forward again, and with John beside him and Alasdair pacing me we marched on to enter Glencoe.

The road ahead of us seemed to run straight towards the high, conical mass of Sgor na Ciche, but just as I thought we must surely fetch up directly against the face of this mountain the road swung sharply to the right. We rounded this bend to enter the glen and I drew a long breath of awe at the sight which opened out before us.

On our left stretched a high, unbroken mountain-wall, crusted with snow and streaked with frozen waterfalls. On our right a line of soaring peaks broke the sky with huge, jagged shapes. The glen was very narrow, and so steeply did the wall of mountain and its facing peaks rise on either side of it that the whole prospect seemed the work of a giant sword cutting a single chain of mountains in half. No human imagination could ever have called up a scene of such grandeur, I thought, and marched on with my head turning from side to side in silent wonder at the strange, wild beauty of it.

Alasdair's voice brought me back to the business in hand.

'My wife will be pleasured by your acquaintance, at least, sir,' he was saying. 'She is also a Stewart of Appin.'

I was pleased to hear this for I had liked the look of Alasdair himself when I saw him first. Both sons, it had struck me then, resembled the fierce old warrior who had burst in on me at the Spur Gate guard-house a month previously, though neither had his massive build nor his extraordinary height. Of the two, however, Alasdair was the more like him. John, moreover, had a quiet very composed presence, whereas Alasdair had the same hawk-like fierceness of eye which had made me admire the old man even while I trembled before him.

I made suitable reply to Alasdair's remark and then inquired the name of the hamlet we had passed through at the entrance to the glen.

'That was Carnoch, at the western end of the glen,' he told me. 'My brother and I have our dwelling there. The hamlet ahead of us now is Inverrigan, and as you go eastwards down the glen there is also Achnacon. Further east still is Achtriochtan – but there are few people living there at the moment for it is too exposed to the eastern wind to be pleasant in winter. Most of the clan are gathered now at Achnacon and Inverrigan and Carnoch.'

'And MacIan, the Chief – where does he stay?'

Alasdair laughed. 'He has a fine mansion at Carnoch but he has given that over to my brother John for he says that he does not like to be tied to any one house – and that a big one! He stays where it suits him for the moment and just now he has decided to winter at his farmhouse in Glen Muidhe. You will see it presently.'

We marched on through Inverrigan. Hardly a soul was to be seen among the little houses which made up the hamlet, but I felt that many eyes watched us as we passed. It was the same at Achnacon, farther eastwards down the glen, and here Glenlyon drew the troop to a halt. Calling Sergeant Barbour forward he told him to hold the men in order and then, with the Chief's sons still accompanying us, we officers continued on our way.

This now led up a narrow glen opening out between two of the mountain masses forming the southern wall of Glencoe.

This little glen, Alasdair informed me, was called Glen Muidhe, and he also named for me the mountains flanking it.

'The round-topped mountain on your right is called Meall Mor,' he explained. 'The name means, "the big round hill". And on your left there you have the highest mountain mass in Glencoe – Bidean nam Bian, "The Pinnacle of the Peaks".'

We marched on, the track under our feet rising only slightly at first and then growing steeper the further we headed up Glen Muidhe. To the left of us a torrent of water roared down between the walls of a narrow rock-fissure in the bed of the glen. The sound of it plunging from waterfall to waterfall was loud enough to make conversation difficult, and with only occasional further words exchanged we covered the mile or so of track that lay between the entrance to Glen Muidhe and MacIan's house.

It was not, by any standards, a grand house I thought, looking round at the smoke-blackened beams supporting the low roof of heather-thatch and the crudely-made wooden furniture. However, the drinking-cups that were set before us were of solid silver and of a most exquisite workmanship of design. The wine poured into them was the best French claret, and when Lady Glencoe set my cup before me it was with a hand bearing jewelled rings of great beauty and value.

So struck was I by these rings that I stared at them longer than was courteous, and then was embarrassed to see Lieutenant Lindsay do the same, but with an expression of such open covetousness on his face that I was shocked by it. Fortunately, Lady Glencoe noticed nothing of all this, and continued to speak pleasantly to us younger officers while Glenlyon made his explanations to MacIan.

The old man listened, frowning, with his chin sunk on to his chest. Occasionally his fierce old eyes darted a wary upward glance at Glenlyon but our Company Commander was not put out by this. He rattled on about the inconvenient conditions at the Fort, his regret at being billeted on the Glencoe Macdonalds in the scarcity-time of winter, and his determination to make the imposition as light as possible. He referred several times, also, to the slight bond of kinship between his own wife and Alasdair's, and eventually MacIan seemed to be convinced of our harmlessness and good intentions to him and his clan.

He rose to his feet and with a dignity that made Glenlyon's chatter seemed vulgar by comparison he said, 'It is yourself that is welcome then, Glenlyon – you and your men. Our best hospitality is yours to command and my sons will assist you to billet your men. Your good self and your officers may choose your own accommodation.'

'Then 'tis Inverrigan I choose,' Glenlyon told him, 'for that is right in the heart of Glencoe and I would be right in the heart of your people, MacIan.'

The old man bowed in answer to this gracious speech. 'My sons and three other close kinsmen of mine will dine with me tonight,' he said. 'You will be giving us your company then also, gentlemen.'

The which, I reflected as we all trooped outside again, was not so much an invitation as a command. MacIan might be the Chief of a clan of only some five hundred souls but he was still, nevertheless, an absolute ruler whose lightest word was law!

Billeting of the men took us till nightfall of that day. Each house in the various hamlets was allotted one, two, or three soldiers as their accommodation allowed, and several families in each hamlet were also required to vacate their homes and move in with neighbours so that we could have empty buildings for use as guard-houses. I thought it something of a shame that whole families should be thus displaced, but when I mentioned this opinion to Glenlyon he only grinned at me. His voice had a vicious sound to it, however, as he said, 'I see you are a very tender-hearted young man, Ensign Stewart. You must take care not to let that tenderness stand in the way of your doing the King's duty.'

I was both puzzled by this unlooked-for rebuke and offended by it. 'Sir,' I retorted, 'you may rest assured you will not find me tender to the King's enemies!'

Glenlyon stared at me, his grin now faded to a look of cold speculation. He said slowly, 'Indeed, Ensign Stewart? It relieves my mind to hear you say so.'

He paused for a long moment with his eyes still fixed on me, then in a different, brisker tone he added. 'The guard-houses are an essential part of our occupation of the glen, Stewart. Therefore, I pray you not to annoy me with further discussion on the subject.'

He turned away then, leaving me with the feeling that I had blundered somehow with my first remark and wondering uneasily how it was that such a sharp exchange about loyalty had been provoked by such a slight expression of sympathy on my part.

We were helped throughout in our task of billeting the men, by the Chief's sons and also by the three cadet gentry of the clan who were to dine at MacIan's house with us later that evening. These Macdonald gentlemen, known as Inverrigan, Achnacon, and Achtriochtan from the lands they held on tack, or lease, from MacIan were of particular assistance to us, and the billeting went forward all the more smoothly in consequence of their help. Indeed, the only incident which marred the harmony of our arrangements, was not of Macdonald making.

It was an unpleasant affair involving a young girl who was Achtriochtan's daughter and who came sobbing to her father with the complaint that Ensign Lundie had tried to force his attentions on her. Achtriochtan's face grew black as thunder and so did Glenlyon's, listening while the girl spoke.

'Dhé!' he muttered angrily aside to Lindsay. 'Does the young fool not realize she is a gentleman's daughter!'

Since I had been nurtured in the belief that a young woman was entitled to protection against unwelcome attentions, whatever her station, this struck me as being a somewhat twisted view of Lundie's behaviour. Moreover, the girl's sobs and her evident distress were touching to witness, and the distaste I felt for my loutish fellow-Ensign was increased as a result of the sight.

The matter was taken out of Glenlyon's hands, however, for Achtriochtan returned from his report of it to the Chief with the order that all the daughters of the cadet gentry, together with the Chief's own daughter, were to remove immediately to the eastern end of the glen where there were few houses and none of them with soldiers billeted in them.

There were no ladies present at supper that night, in consequence of this, except for Lady Glencoe herself presiding over the table. However, galled as I was at Lundie for having thus abused our honour as officers, I still preferred this masculine company which set us free to talk solely of hunting and military matters. I fell into conversation with Alasdair on these subjects and was deep in talk with him when I heard MacIan's voice rise loudly over the other voices around us.

He was saying something about Colin Campbell of Ardkinglas, the Sheriff of Inveraray. I turned to look up the table to him, and seeing that everyone else now had their attention fixed on the old man I hoped that he was about to speak of that night he had ridden to Inveraray to swear the oath, for various accounts of what had happened to him had been current in the Fort since then and I was eager to learn the true version. Nor was I disappointed in my hopes, for as soon as he saw that he had all our attention, MacIan launched forth.

'It was the snow-wind that was blowing hard that night, you will remember,' he said, 'and man, but it was a terrible storm that was in it! I rode that storm blind for I could scarce open my eyes against the weight of the snow that was beating on them. My gillies, poor lads, were frozen to the marrow of their bones, and altogether it was only a mile southwards we could make in every hour that passed. Still we pressed on all that night and all the next day, and with darkness coming down for the second sight and the storm abating, we passed Balcardine Castle. And oh, it was myself that was a sorry man to see that place!'

He paused, scowling at the memory of Balcardine, and then burst out, 'Yon fellow Drummond is a Lowland pig! D'ye know the insult he put upon me – *me*, MacIan of Glencoe!'

Glenlyon had lowered his eyes to the table at the mention of Captain Drummond's name. No one answered the old man and he continued indignantly, 'It was himself that was in command of the Balcardine garrison that night, and he was not just content with sending out a troop of his fellows to over-power me and my gillies so that we could be brought before him – to answer for ourselves as he called it. He was after throwing me into a filthy dungeon at Balcardine and keeping me there like a common criminal for twenty-four hours!'

Lady Glencoe stretched out a sympathetic hand to her husband. Her jewelled rings flashed in the candle-light and I noticed Lindsay fix covetous eyes on them again as she soothed MacIan.

'But even he could not be setting his face entirely against the safe-conduct Colonel Hill had given you,' she said.

'Aye, aye, that is so,' MacIan agreed. 'But all that time had been lost to me before I won free of him and the next day the blizzard rose up in my face even stronger than it had been before. A miracle of Heaven it was that we survived it at all, for the danger of being buried alive in the drifts in the valleys was on us, and so we had to scramble along on the hill-slopes where the wind had swept them bare of snow. Small wonder, then, that I did not reach Inveraray in time!'

Glenlyon looked up. 'A remarkable tale of courage and perseverance, MacIan,' he said so heartily that I doubted if anyone but myself noticed how adroitly his comment enabled him to avoid any reference to the insulting behaviour of Captain Drummond.

The old Chief acknowledged the compliment with an inclination of his massive head, and Glenlyon added piously, 'And by God's grace all ended well – for of course the Government has accepted your oath even though it was sworn after the time-limit.'

'Aye, Colin of Ardkinglas had kindness for me, though he is a Campbell,' MacIan admitted. 'He was after writing a letter to the Privy Council telling them it was no fault of mine that I was late in taking the oath, and saying that I must therefore be brought into the King's mercy – or I would not be resting easy now with the red soldiers in my glen!'

He drew himself up and looked proudly at Glenlyon. 'So may you rest easy in Glencoe, sir,' he said, 'for all you are Campbells among Macdonalds! It is my word that has gone out to my clansmen that you have come in peace and are to be treated hospitably. The clansmen are as children to their Chief, and my children will obey me.'

I murmured my thanks along with the rest and then, because it had puzzled me, I could not resist asking, 'Sir, why did you not come in to swear the oath earlier in the year, while the weather was still clement?'

MacIan shot me one of his fierce, frowning looks. 'I had sworn an earlier oath to another king –' he growled '– the one that earned me the name of rebel. Yet still it bound me. I could take no other oath till I was freed from that earlier allegiance, and the envoy who brought the message so freeing me was delayed in his arrival.'

I bowed my acknowledgment of his explanation thinking that, rebel or no, a loyalty that bade a man risk life and lands in order to keep his word was worthy of respect.

MacIan continued to eye me for a moment and then he said. '*You* were courteous to me, young sir, the night I came seeking admittance to the Fort. And you fronted me bravely, too, for all I put you in fear of my sword being laid about you.'

Smiling I acknowledged, 'I *was* afraid of you, sir, but I still had my duty as an officer to do.'

'That is Kenneth Stewart of Eilidh's voice speaking in you now,' he told me. 'I would know you for a son of his anywhere.'

'We were well acquainted with your father before he left Appin to go soldiering in foreign parts,' Lady Glencoe added gently, 'and sorry we were when your great-aunt sent us the sad news of his death.'

'By your leave, madam,' I said. ' 'Twas no sad news.'

MacIan's eyes widened with interest as I spoke. 'So, boy?' he asked quietly. 'How *did* he die?'

'Bravely sir, leading his men into action against superior numbers.'

The old Chief's piercing gaze held mine for a few seconds after I said this and then he nodded and half-smiled as if satisfied by what he saw.

'You have the right of it, Robert Stewart,' he said. 'Courage needs no mourners!'

There was a slight pause and then Glenlyon said briskly, 'Well MacIan, we must be off. We have guards to set before we sleep tonight.'

MacIan looked up, startled. 'Guards? In *my* glen?'

'The regulations demand it,' Glenlyon said apologetically. 'The drill must be kept up and the guards set the very same as if we were in the Fort. The Army is bound by regulations, MacIan – as I know to my sorrow!'

'Aye, Glenlyon. I fear me a rattling fellow like yourself will be taking ill out on King William's discipline,' MacIan replied with a sudden twinkle of humour in his fierce eyes.

The rest of the company had risen one by one as Glenlyon spoke, and now as he laughed in response to MacIan's jest we moved off towards the door. John, the eldest son, stopped us on our way there to invite us courteously to take a morning draught the following day with his brother and himself. Calling their goodnights the tacksmen Inverrigan, Achtriochtan and Achnacon went ahead of us while we spoke with John, leaving Glenlyon, Lundie, Lindsay and myself to walk as a group back to our billet in Inverrigan's house, in the hamlet of Inverrigan itself.

It was a splendid night, the kind of night that only occurs in winter when the clear frostiness of the air makes the stars seem very sharp and bright against the blackness of the sky. Sound carries well on such a night. I heard clearly what Lindsay said at one point, even though his voice was then only a murmur a few paces behind me and on my left.

'The cubs are still with the old fox.'

Then Glenlyon's voice, also a murmur, replying to him, *'The old fox is quiet enough in his den. 'Tis the young cub that still sniffs the air for danger.'*

I walked on steadily, making no sign that I had heard this curious interchange, but I thought about it later as I went the round of the guard-detail at Inverrigan. *'The old fox and his cubs'* – that was MacIan and his sons, of course. And the young cub sniffing the air for danger was Alasdair with his suspicious attitude to us. So I reasoned and it seemed to me a curiously derisive way to refer to our hosts, especially when I remembered the smiles and polite talk exchanged over the supper-table that night.

I had no taste for such two-faced behaviour and I wished

that Lindsay and Glenlyon were not senior to me in rank so that I could have said so frankly to them. Beyond that, the matter seemed of little moment, and I did not dwell further on it.

4 Officers' rounds

My first impression of Glencoe stayed with me as we settled down to our life there, and each morning when I stepped from my quarters at Inverrigan I saw the wild beauty of the glen with the same eyes of wonder as on the day we had first entered it. Nor was I slow to appreciate that a valley so narrow and so completely walled in by precipitous mountains provided the Macdonalds with an impregnable defence against any attack from outside Glencoe.

It was a perfect example of a stronghold which nothing except treachery from inside could overwhelm, and with the complete loyalty to one another on which the whole of the clan system was based this was a hazard the Macdonalds need never even take into account.

Ideally as it was situated for military defence, however, Glencoe was also fertile as I discovered when I had leisure to explore the nine miles of its length stretching from the Moor of Rannoch at its eastern end to Loch Leven and the mountain of Sgor na Ciche at its western-most point. There were well-harvested fields of oats and barley on the valley floor. Herds of fat black cattle grazed the rich pastures on either bank of the Coe, the river which watered the glen, and the rocky stream of the river itself swarmed with an abundance of sea-trout. Besides this, as Alasdair had told me on our first evening there, there was good hunting of roe deer in the birch coverts at Inverrigan and Achnacon, and of red deer on the mountain slopes.

Glenlyon had spoken truly when he said that the people of Glencoe did not lack for good winter provender, and his prophecy that we would live fat there was quickly proved true for the Macdonalds did not stint of their best either to us officers or to the common soldiery.

We settled down quickly into life in the glen. The roster of guard-duty was made up and a stretch of flat ground at the hamlet of Achnacon was chosen as a drill-ground. There were sports and recreations at this place also, and the men of the glen put forward a shinty team to contest with our own Company team at this game so beloved of all Highlanders. Card parties and supper parties were arranged for the officers at the homes of the Chief and his sons, and among the common people – as I discovered on my rounds of guard inspection – there was much telling of tales, piping and other such entertainments for passing the long winter evenings.

For my own part, I felt most at home in the house of Alasdair. I stood too much in awe of old MacIan to be truly at ease in his presence, and when he frowned – as he always did when Glenlyon grew too tipsy after supper for good manners' sake, I constantly expected some explosion of wrathful dignity from him. As for John's house at Carnoch, this was the Chief's mansion Alasdair had mentioned to me at our first encounter. It was a large house well-plenished with good furnishings, and though I liked the atmosphere of it and the quiet good-nature of John himself I had few tastes in common with him. Thus it was with Alasdair and his wife, Mistress Elspeth, that I spent my kindest times in Glencoe for Alasdair was as willing to talk of war as I was myself, he shared my passion for hunting also and Mistress Elspeth had a merry nature that gave good company.

She was eager to hear all the gossip of Appin from me, but having been so seldom there in the past year I could give her little except my cousin Elizabeth's troubles with Great-Aunt Euphemia. Woman-like, she seized on this immediately and squeezed as much juice from the subject as she could. I was greatly amused at her chatter and would have shown my amusement at it much more than I did if Alasdair had not kept so grave a face over it, and one day as we walked together to the drill-ground at Achnacon I came back to the subject with him.

'Tell me, Alasdair Og,' I challenged, 'why have you been keeping so long a face over that piece of women's wedding-gossip I gave Mistress Elspeth?'

He looked sideways at me as if calculating how much to say and then remarked. 'You have not been long in the Highlands, Robert, or you would know that no one ever mixed his fortunes with those of the Earl of Breadalbane without taking a deal of thought beforehand.'

'But Elizabeth is marrying some kinsman of his – not the Earl himself,' I protested.

'Breadalbane is only one step lower in rank in the Campbell clan than the Duke of Argyll, the Chief himself,' Alasdair said deliberately. 'Moreover, Clan Campbell is the most powerful in the land and Breadalbane has a finger in every one of its pies. Your cousin will achieve wealth and position under his wing, Robert, but there is poor chance of her ever knowing happiness.'

I could not in the least see why this should be the case and said so rather heatedly. Alasdair gave me a long and searching look and at last he said:

'Now mark this well, Robert Stewart. Breadalbane is a rogue, a cheat and a double-cheat. When William and James fought for the crown in 1688 he played one side against the other yet made money and gained lands from both of them. There is no treachery too low for him to stoop to, no person he has power over that he does not use as a tool to work for him. This young man your cousin is to marry is such a one as Breadalbane uses, and therefore she – if she loves honour at all – has no happy future before her.'

I walked on beside him in silence, too dismayed by all this to make any comment, and after a few moments Alasdair added:

'Your great-aunt knows all this but she, too, loves power and she is evidently too blinded by ambition for your cousin to refuse the match that has been offered for her.'

'You sound as bitter, Alasdair Og,' I said, 'as if you had some personal quarrel with Breadalbane.'

Alasdair did not answer this for a moment or two and then, reluctantly, he admitted. 'There *is* a matter of dispute between Breadalbane and my clan.'

There was another silence and then he added angrily, 'Breadalbane has touched my father's honour. He called him thief!'

Wisely, as I thought, I made no reply to this for the field of another's honour is delicate ground to tread. We walked on together, each thinking his own thoughts, and came to a halt eventually beside the drill-ground at Achnacon where Sergeant Barbour was putting a section of the men through their musket-drill.

I disliked Sergeant Barbour as much as I had ever done. Indeed, with every day of our stay in the glen my dislike of him increased, for his boorish manner was in strong contrast to the courtesy of our Macdonald hosts. Moreover, the more I saw of the man the more I was convinced that he was what my father had always referred to contemptuously as 'a butcher' – the type of man who had become a soldier for no other reason than that he took a pleasure in killing men. There was something about those pebble-hard dark eyes of his that warned me of this, and whenever I thought of it and heard the almost beast-like snarl of his voice commanding the men it was enough to set a small shiver of horror lifting the hair on the back of my neck.

I felt that same little shiver of horror go over me then as I listened to his words of command cutting hard and sharp as shots through the clear mountain air:

'Draw your rammers and shorten – One, Two! Insert in barrel, ram home – One, Two! Recover rammers and shorten – One Two! Return rammers – One, Two, Three! Present and Fire – One!'

'They move like wooden men through these motions,' Alasdair's voice broke into the pattern of shouted command.

'They are meant to do so,' I said shortly, not willing to enter into a discussion of the training with anyone outside the Regiment. Alasdair looked at me curiously then his gaze wandered back to Sergeant Barbour.

'There is one man,' he observed, 'who knows how to keep himself aloof from others. Achnacon tells me that he never enters into conversation in his billet but simply eats what is set before him and, if there is no further work for him to do, goes straight to bed.'

'Except when he is conferring with Glenlyon,' I added, and then could have bitten my tongue off for it was no business of Alasdair's that the Senior Sergeant seemed to spend an undue amount of time in colloquy with the Captain of the Company.

Alasdair made no comment on my slip of the tongue. Instead he began to talk about hunting and I arranged to ask permission to hunt with him two days thence.

'I have some winter ploughing in Carnoch that must be done while the ground stays soft in this fine weather,' Alasdair explained the delay, and we took our leave of one another at Inverrigan on that note.

I went back to my billet feeling that Glencoe was a good place to live in and that its people were no barbarians despite their simple way of life. Many of them, I was discovering, had some knowledge of English in addition to their native Gaelic. The Chief and the other gentry of the clan spoke English well despite the peculiar Gaelic phrasing they lent to it, and they also had a fair knowledge of French.

It was a pity, I thought, that Lieutenant Lindsay and Ensign Lundie had only English to their command, for Glenlyon could talk in Gaelic with the Chief and his sons while both Lady Glencoe and her men-folk enjoyed many conversations in French with me. Yet it might not have made much difference, after all, however many tongues these two were versed in. They seemed naturally a surly pair despite all the friendly advances that had been made to them.

And yet again, I thought, they seemed to have plenty to say to one another – although their conversation always died away whenever I came near! They were a strange pair altogether, I decided. And Glenlyon was strange too, with his wittiness when sober and his loutishness when he was in wine. I thought for a few moments longer about this, and then dismissing it from my mind, I picked up the off-duty roster and began to select the names of the team for the next shinty match.

I scanned the list of available men and noted among the names that of Private MacEachern, the man who saw visions. I had never seen him play myself but he had asked for a place in the team and Corporal Kennedy had told me that he was a handy man with the *caman* – the stick the players wielded so fearsomely in the game of shinty. I wrote his name into the team and smiled to myself as I did so, thinking how pleased he would be to find himself chosen. He had been a smarter soldier since the night he had let MacIan past him at the Spur Gate and I had given him a warning instead of the flogging he deserved, and having come to the conclusion that he was truly just a great simpleton, I had continued to do my best for the poor fellow since then. This small reward, I thought, would encourage him to continue his efforts to be a good soldier.

I was still writing when my host, Inverrigan, entered the house carrying a basket of fat sea-trout. Glenlyon followed him in, rubbing his hands with pleasure at the sight of the fish.

'They eat like salmon,' Inverrigan told me. 'Firm-fleshed and as tasty a fish as ever came out of the water, you will find them.'

'Aye, the thin kale and porridge of our rations at the Fort draw further and further back in the memory with every day we spend in your glen, Inverrigan,' Glenlyon said jovially. 'We'll have a glass of wine to keep the cold out, will we, man?'

Glenlyon drank too much – too much for decency's sake and perhaps even too much for military security, I thought, watching him then and later on also while we sat at supper with Inverrigan and his family. I felt discomfited by the inanity of some of the remarks the wine put on his tongue, and was glad to escape that night to my duty of making the round of the guard-posts.

Lundie and Lindsay came out with me, one to carry out the inspection at Carnoch where Sergeant Hendrie was in charge of the billets and the other to do the same at Achnacon where Sergeant Barbour was in charge. I stood for several moments after they had gone, looking up at the brilliance of the stars and thinking strange, muddled thoughts about that odd man, Captain Robert Campbell of Glenlyon.

Was he a fool or a wise man? Cruel or kindly? A gentleman or an oaf? He had shown himself to be something of all these in turn and yet none of these descriptions fitted his character exactly. What was his real nature, I wondered, and thought I could no more tell what it was than I could have guessed the distance that separated the stars from the mountain peaks of the glen. And so I shook these thoughts away from me and carried on with my duty of inspecting the guard.

There were three guard-points at Inverrigan, one only a few

yards from the officers' billet in the house of Inverrigan himself and the other two placed one at either end of the hamlet. The nearby one was only a small, single-roomed dwelling which Glenlyon had turned into a check-point where the rosters were kept and reports made from the various sections. There was only a Corporal on duty there, as a rule, and having verified briefly from him that no one had reported sick and that all at Inverrigan was quiet so far, I walked quickly over to the first of the main guard-posts.

All was in order there. The sentries challenged me alertly, and there were no signs of drunkenness or gambling in the orderly room. Satisfied, I walked through the village to the second guard-post. It was in the same good order as the first, and my tour of inspection now finished, I began the walk back to my billet.

It was not yet very late and the people of the glen were still not a-bed. Lights showed in most of the houses I passed and from some of them came the sound of voices and occasionally a snatch of pipe-music or singing. It was pleasant to hear the common people thus enjoying themselves, and on the impulse I stopped at one house, pulled the door gently open and looked in.

There was a group of people seated round the hearth – the man of the house and his wife, several children of various ages, and an elderly man who was swaying back and forward in his seat and reciting something in Gaelic.

I made my entrance so softly that the group round the hearth did not notice me at first, their attention all being concentrated on the old man's recital. I had no Gaelic, of course, but I caught the name 'MacIan' several times which made me curious, and when the old man noticed me at last and stopped in some confusion at the sight of me I said:

'No, no, grandfather, do not stop your tale – but tell me first what story this is you are telling of MacIan.'

The old man had no English, however, and it was the woman of the house who said shyly, 'Sir, he is telling the tale of Angus of Clan Donald, the first man to hold the title of Lord of the Isles, and of his son Ian Og – or Young John, as you would call him in English. And he is telling it to the children so that they should know that the Chiefs of the Mac-donalds of Glencoe are all descended in direct line through Ian Og from the Lord of the Isles himself. And that is why our Chief today – like all the Chiefs who have gone before him, is called MacIan – the son of John.'

A strange people, I thought to myself as I thanked her and withdrew. There they sat in their rough-woven tartans in the peat-smoke that filled their crude dwelling-places, telling tales to impress on their children the nobility of their descent. For the clan was one people, was it not? And since the Chief was nobly descended, so also were the people for the same blood ran in their veins as ran in his.

Just over a year ago when I first came to Scotland I would have laughed at the absurdity of such pride, but now I was not so sure that it was a matter for laughter. These people – even the poorest of them – had a dignity about them that called for an equal courtesy on my part.

I walked on feeling that I had come to a better under-standing of the clan system than all my father's explanations of it during the years of my upbringing on foreign soil had ever given me, and was presently stopped again by the sound of laughter coming from another house. A voice roared out something in Gaelic in the midst of the laughter, and recogni-zing Private MacEachern's tones and wondering what on earth the great simpleton was up to now, I pushed open the door of this house also.

The same sort of family group as in the other house was seated round the hearth here also, but this time Private MacEachern was the centre of it. The man of the house and his wife were seated in the background. MacEachern had a very small child on his knee. A boy of thirteen or so hung over the back of his chair and a smaller boy who might have been about seven years old leant against his knee.

MacEachern was roaring in Gaelic at the top of his voice, making it as gruff as possible, and the children were screaming with laughter at the sound. He stopped, his mouth hanging open in dismay when he saw me, and jumping to his feet he thrust the small child into its mother's arms.

I grinned in spite of myself at his confusion, and said

mildly, 'At ease, MacEachern. I only stopped in to hear the cause of all this merriment.'

'Sir – oh, sir,' he stammered, 'it – it was only a tale for the bairns.'

'About a giant!' the older boy said with shining eyes, 'a giant in the olden times. That was his voice the red soldier was making just now.'

'What happened to this giant?' I asked MacEachern teasingly. 'Was he a terror to the land?'

'Sometimes, sir, but he was a – he was also a very trusting sort of fellow,' MacEachern stammered, and then ran on nervously as if he could not stop talking once he had started, '—and one night when he was sleeping some cunning people crept up on him and cut off his head and stole his great sword that was called a sword of light because it was so bright and sharp. And this they could do because the giant was not cunning enough himself to think they could make such a plan against him.'

The smaller of the two boys came thrusting up to me then saying something in Gaelic and holding up a tattered chapbook for me to see.

The man of the house put forward a hand to draw the child back to him and said apologetically, 'It is a Book of Tales he has, sir. Father Cameron gave it to him to study when he found the boy very forward at his letters and he is so proud of it he will show it to everyone.'

It was a crudely-illustrated *Lives of the Saints* the child was holding out to me with a text badly printed in Latin. As I glanced briefly at it, it reminded me that the Glencoe Macdonalds were of the Roman Catholic faith, and I also recalled hearing it said that they were ever staunch in their support of the Old Church.

' 'Tis a very fine thing for a child to have,' I told the father courteously, 'and I pray pardon for having interrupted your family gathering.'

I turned to go, and rising from his seat the man of the house came to the door with me. His hand on the latch to pull the door open, he asked,

'You are son to Kenneth Stewart of Eilidh, are you not?'

I nodded, and the Macdonald said quietly, 'Himself was a fine soldier. A proper man, indeed!'

I stepped through the door with a murmured word of thanks for this unexpected tribute to my father and the man said, 'It was his due. I knew him when he was a young man in Appin, and I am proud to have had his son under my roof.'

'Thank you, and a good night to you,' I told him, and walked back to my billet feeling so puffed up by this little interchange that I seemed to feel inches taller than my natural height!

'Ah, welcome back, Stewart – we missed you. You have been a long time away,' Glenlyon greeted my entrance.

He was seated facing Inverrigan over the dining-table. The dishes had been cleared off it leaving only the wine-decanter and some glasses. A document of some kind lay on the table among the glasses, one corner of it lying wet in a little pool of spilt wine. Inverrigan looked worried and he was drumming nervously on this document with the tips of his fingers, but from his greeting to me Glenlyon appeared to have drunk himself into a jovial frame of mind.

I matched his good humour with my own, and as I began unbuckling my sword-belt replied to him, 'I was detained by a tale, sir – the tale of a giant!'

Glenlyon swung round with a quizzical glance at me. 'The devil you were!'

'Yes, sir. I stopped in at a house in the village and listened to the story of a foolish giant who fell asleep too trustingly. And then the little people of the land crept up on him and cut off his head and stole his sword of many battles!'

Glenlyon stared at me, the enquiring look on his face giving way slowly to amusement. A rumble of laughter began in his chest and rose upwards to explode in a great guffaw. I laughed with him, but Inverrigan only smiled and looked uncertainly from one to the other of us. Glenlyon continued to laugh – excessively, it seemed to me, for such a slender jest, and to say between gasps of his laughter:

'Oh, the foolish fellow ... Fell asleep, did he? ... Too trusting, eh? ... Oh lord – there was a fate deserved ...!'

The joke spent at last he looked owlishly across at Inverrigan and said,

'Come man, why can *you* not laugh and be cheerful? Your bit of paper is in order, I tell you. And Achnacon and Achtriochtan will say the same to you if you ask them. *They* were satisfied to be sworn by Colonel Hill. Why cannot you be the same?'

Inverrigan turned to me. 'What do *you* think, Mr Stewart?'

I had no knowledge of what they were discussing and could only shake my head and tell him so apologetically.

'The trouble is this,' Glenlyon said impatiently. 'There was a Proclamation of Indemnity issued to the rebel clans some months earlier than the one under which MacIan himself took the oath of allegiance. The cadet gentry of the clan – including Inverrigan here – all took the oath of allegiance under that earlier proclamation and it was Colonel Hill himself who received that oath, for military commanders had the power to do so at the time.'

He leaned forward and flicked at the wine-stained document on the table. 'See, here is Inverrigan's assurance of indemnity writ in the Colonel's hand. And yet he is worrying whether it is enough to protect him against Government action, and declaring he will only feel safe if he takes the oath again before the Sheriff, as MacIan did.'

'It was MacIan advised us of the wisdom of doing so,' Inverrigan said quickly. 'He said we could not trust—'

He stopped, his hand flying to his mouth, his face appalled at the indiscretion he had been about to commit.

'Could not trust whom?' Leaning forward over the table Glenlyon menaced him with wine-reddened eyes. 'The Government, Inverrigan? The red soldiers? Glenlyon's troop – your own guests? Is that why you are so worried? You think we will turn on you, maybe?'

Bristling with outrage, he rose to his feet violently pushing his chair away with the movement. Inverrigan rose more slowly, reaching for the paper and folding it as he rose. He looked from it to Glenlyon. His face flushed and then went pale again as they confronted one another, but when he spoke at last it was with great dignity.

'I am satisfied by what you say, Glenlyon, and I ask pardon humbly for even thinking of treachery from a man who has eaten my salt.'

I had listened to this exchange with very mixed feelings. Inverrigan, I could see, was a man genuinely worried. And yet, I had myself been so offended by his implication of treachery from us that my sympathies were wholly with Glenlyon in his burst of outrage. Now, however, Inverrigan had made full amends and so I felt justified in exclaiming, 'Handsomely spoken, sir!'

Glenlyon glanced at me. His frowning brow grew smooth again. A smile began to quiver round his mouth and turning back to Inverrigan he clapped him heartily on the shoulder.

'Put it behind you, Inverrigan!' he cried. 'Come, we will have a hand at the cards to help us forget this nonsense!'

'With all my heart, Glenlyon,' Inverrigan said eagerly. 'I will plenish the wine and fetch the pack while I am about it.'

He lifted the almost-empty decanter from the table and hurried out of the room. Glenlyon tossed off what remained in his glass and looked across at me, his lips pressed together and stretched in a smile, his eyes half-closed.

'You are quite a diplomat, young Stewart,' he remarked. 'Will you take a hand at the cards with us?'

I was sleepy and the prospect of an hour – perhaps two hours, of cards did not attract me and so I said politely, 'I am tired, sir. I beg you to excuse me.'

He nodded, and smiled his closed-lips smile again. I thought that it combined with his sleepy-lidded eyes to give him the expression of a huge, contented cat, and for a fleeting moment I could understand why Inverrigan had been on the point of implying treachery to him. Cats were sly and treacherous beasts, and if Glenlyon had looked at Inverrigan with that expression while the Colonel's assurance of indemnity was being discussed . . .!

It was a ridiculous, fanciful thought of course. As I settled down for the night on my pallet of straw and heather I smiled inwardly at the absurdity of it and told myself that I must have been infected for the moment by the tale-spinning fantasies of MacEachern and his simple-minded kind.

5 A spy –

The deer-hunt I had discussed with Alasdair took place, as arranged, two days from this time and I wore Highland garb for the first time in my life for the event. I could not be accepted into the hunt otherwise, Alasdair informed me, since the clan huntsmen would never consent to share the chase except with those who conformed to all their traditional usages.

It was Alasdair also who supplied me with the long length of tartan cloth they called a 'plaid' and showed me how to kilt it in pleats that were belted round my waist, leaving the free end of the plaid to be thrown up over my left shoulder and caught again on my chest by a jewelled pin. To wear with this plaid he gave me a pair of the single-soled shoes they called 'brogans', made of cowhide and punched with holes which would allow any water encountered to enter and run out freely again. These were laced calf-high on my bare legs and were more suited to damp terrain than my ordinary boots which would have retained all the water soaked up by their leather.

Thus attired, armed with a borrowed bow and a quiverful of arrows and very aware of the strange feel of my garb, I went with him to meet the hunting-party by the tacksman's house at Achnacon at first light on the day of the hunt. The tacksman, Achnacon himself, came out with his servants to give us a morning draught and while we drank this down I eyed the men of the hunting party.

There were about forty all told, half of them armed with bows and arrows with the rest carrying wooden staves, and I thought it would be difficult to find anywhere such a body of well-built men. All except a few younger ones looked to be about twenty or so years of age. They were all tall with the spare, lean-muscled build of athletes, broad of shoulder and long in the leg. Their features were all cast in the hawk-faced Macdonald mould and they all had the dark, fierce-glinting eyes which I had come to recognize as a sign of the Clan Donald blood.

A little apart from the group they made stood another one of boys and older men, and these held by the reins the ponies which would carry the deer-carcases back to the glen. Alasdair noted how my look skimmed over these bearers to return admiringly to the huntsmen and he said proudly:

'There is not one among our hunters who could not outrun a horse on a day's travel!'

It was a boast that was easy to believe and I hoped devoutly that I would not be found wanting in such company!

I had not yet been told where the hunt would take place. I glanced behind me at the sheer unbroken mountain wall that formed the north side of the glen and thought that deer could hardly have climbed these crags let alone find a living on them. It must be to the south the hunt would go, I decided, for only in the south wall of the glen were there any passes through the mountains. Glen Muidhe, where MacIan had his winter home, was one of these passes. The other two were the Lairig Gartain and the Lairig Eilde, but they were four miles down the glen from Achnacon whereas Glen Muidhe stood almost exactly opposite that hamlet.

'Is it Glen Muidhe we hunt?' I asked Alasdair.

He nodded. 'Aye, the going there is nothing like as steep as it is through the Lairig Gartain or the Lairig Eilde, and we do not want to kill you on your first day out with us!'

He smiled as he said this, with a friendliness that took any sting out of the words, and then with a wave of his arm he signalled the hunt to move off. The group of tall young men surged towards Glen Muidhe at the trot, followed at a slower pace by the men and boys with their garrons. I had been about to ask what the method of the hunt would be but when I saw the pace these lean young hunters were setting I judged it wiser to save my breath. I broke into a trot beside Alasdair and the hunt headed rapidly on up Glen Muidhe.

For well over a mile we maintained our starting pace, the hunters with their bows and the beaters with their staves keeping a compact formation along the track that climbed to the Chief's house. Here, where the track ended and the ground on either side of the torrent running down the glen grew suddenly very boggy, the men began to deploy into what I took to be their hunting positions.

All except a few of the bearers spread out in single-line formation across the width of the glen, and one by one were gradually lost to view among the folds and ridges of the ground between its retaining mountain-walls. The bowmen and the remaining beaters climbed rapidly up the lower slopes of Meall Mor, the mountain on our right, and forged onwards up the glen.

Our pace was not slowed by the altered contour of our route for the huntsmen now changed their jog-trot to a quick, loping stride that carried them easily over ridge and dip and stone, and where the steep side of the hill was broken by outcrops of rock they scrambled quick as cats up one side of it and dropped as easily down on the other. I kept up with them, grateful for the custom that had taken the constriction of my military uniform from me and given me the freedom of the Highland garb instead, but still envying them their apparent effortlessness in a pace that was beginning to cost me dear in sweat.

A half-mile or so of this kind of progress brought us round the southern shoulder of Meall Mor, and at this point we struck the confluence of another stream with the Glen Muidhe torrent. It came from a little glen running away to the south-west of Glen Muidhe. Alasdair pointed down this side-glen and said smilingly to me:

'You are not five miles from Eilidh and home now, Robert. That little glen is the path to Glen Creran and the rest of the Appin country.'

He summoned two of the beaters and stationed them at the mouth of the side-glen. The rest of us pressed on our way, and now the strategy of the hunt opened out to me.

The sides of Glen Muidhe were growing steeper with every yard we covered, and the glen itself was narrowing. I could hear faintly shouts and whistles coming from below us and I realized that the beaters strung out across the glen were netting it for us. The beaters we had stationed at the little side-glen would prevent any deer that were driven up Glen Muidhe from breaking free in that direction, and no doubt similar precautions had been taken where there were breaks in the mountain-wall of Bidean nam Bian on the far side of the glen. Meanwhile, I guessed, the hunters were making for some point where they would be ahead of the driven deer, and lying in wait for them there they would pick them off with their arrows.

A whistle longer and louder than the rest brought the hunters up suddenly in their tracks. They listened. The whistle was repeated and with a shout of 'Craig Bhan!' Alasdair pointed to a quartz-veined cliff massif glittering white in the sun ahead of us. The hunters broke into a run heading where he pointed and keeping high on the hillside so that they could circle round the far end of the narrow neck of valley walled in by the cliff.

I ran with them though I had neither hope nor expectation of being able to keep up their pace. From ridge to ridge of the broken ground that made up the mountain face they leapt, clearing hollows at a bound, taking jutting rocks in their stride, and nimbly avoiding the hazards of potholes and patches of small stones sliding loosely underfoot.

Alasdair was in the lead, setting a rough course for the rest of the hunters. I found myself sixth in the line that followed, and I think it was only the shame of being seen to drop out by the man behind me that enabled me to keep on running in that position. The plaid of the man running ahead of me was a flicker of tartan swinging in and out of my field of vision. I kept my eyes on his lean-muscled legs flashing bare beneath its flying folds, and somehow I managed to match them step for step and leap for leap. But how I did not lose my footing on such rough terrain and how my pumping heart did not burst altogether with the strain, I shall never know!

Suddenly the line of our flight swung due east and as we swung the running pace changed to a scramble, for now we had reached the plateau that made the summit of Craig Bhan. Two hundred feet beneath us a narrow strip of green made the floor of the corrie formed by the walls of the cliff. We scrambled towards it. The wet soles of my brogans slipped dangerously where the rocks were smooth but I managed to reach the foot of the cliff without mishap and waited, panting, for Alasdair's orders.

The rest of the hunters were running down the corrie and dividing towards either side of it as they ran. Alasdair motioned me with him and ran for the concealment of a tumble of rocks some hundred yards away on the right-hand side of the corrie. I halted and crouched beside him there, and for the first time became aware of the noise drifting up from the open end of the corrie.

It was the shouting and whistling of the beaters I could hear, and mingled faintly with it the swishing and drumming sound of a herd of deer in rapid motion. I whipped out an arrow and fitted it to my bow, noting as I did so that the iron point of the arrow was flanked by hooked barbs which would make it impossible for a deer to shake loose a shot that proved to be only a wounding one. Alasdair saw the glance I gave the barbs and said curtly:

'We do not hunt for sport, but for food. A wounded deer must be run down and killed.'

I nodded and fixed my eyes on the entrance to the corrie. The sound of the hunt was very near.

The deer appeared as a dark, moving blur at the far end of the corrie. As they drew nearer I saw that they were a small stag-herd of about twenty animals running at full stretch in the blind grip of panic.

'Aim for a heart-shot!' Alasdair's voice hissed beside me.

As he spoke the herd leader was brought to a rearing halt, pierced by the arrow of a bowman farther down the corrie from us. Two more animals on the far side of the herd crashed down as the leader fell but the herd thundered on over them. It was now no longer tightly bunched together. As one beast after another fell to an arrow there was stumbling and confusion that allowed some animals to streak ahead of others. I fixed on a heavily-antlered stag running fast on the near side of the herd. It passed us in a brown blur and there was a simultaneous twang from Alasdair's bow and mine as we both shot.

One arrow took the running stag high in the shoulder. The other went home true to the vital mark behind the near foreleg. The stag stumbled, fell, kicked once and then lay still.

'Well shot, Robert!' Alasdair shouted. 'It was your arrow brought him down!'

I fitted another arrow, my heart hammering hard with excitement but my hands steady on the bow. My target this time was a younger animal. I shot and missed, but from somewhere on the other side of the corrie another bowman's arrow took the stag cleanly and it went down in its death-throes.

The few animals which had managed to run the gauntlet of the bowmen had reached the blind end of the corrie. They milled about, making desperate attempts to leap clear up the crags that hemmed them in, but the hunters advanced from their hiding-places and began picking them off one by one.

Twenty yards up the corrie from me a well-antlered stag fell wounded and struggled to rise. The huntsman who had brought it down rushed towards it, dirk in hand to complete the kill, but only a yard from the beast he stumbled over an outcrop of rock and crashed to the ground. His head struck heavily as he went down and he lay still where he had fallen. The stag was not mortally wounded. It heaved itself to its feet and reared up bellowing with rage and pain. Its sharp hooves pawed the air above the huntsman's head, then it struck downwards with them and as it struck I took it with an arrow to the heart. It crashed down falling partly across the huntsman's body.

Both Alasdair and I ran towards him and together we pulled him clear of the stag. His eyes opened when Alasdair spoke rapidly to him in Gaelic. Quickly we examined him and found he was uninjured apart from the blow to the head. We helped him to rise. As we brought him to his feet he looked dazedly from the dead deer to each of us in turn and said something to Alasdair in Gaelic. Alasdair replied to him, gesturing to me while he did so as if to indicate it was my arrow which had brought the stag down.

The young man's face lit up as he listened and when Alasdair had finished speaking he dropped quickly to one knee in front of me, seizing my hand and laying it against his heart while he poured out a flood of Gaelic speech.

Bewildered and embarrassed by this I looked to Alasdair for enlightenment and he translated, smiling. 'You are his brother now and henceforth his heart will beat only for you. No man, saving his Chief only, will command such loyalty from this day as he will have for you, and to this may God and all the saints bear witness.'

I had no such poetic words in which to answer this speech but I managed to stumble through a brief reply which I hoped would meet the case. Alasdair translated again for me and the young man rose to his feet and saluted me gravely before he went off to join his fellows.

They were gathering in twos and threes round the carcases of the deer. The beaters were coming up to join them and already some had begun the work of 'gralloching' as they called the gutting of the carcases. I made to go and bear a hand with this work but Alasdair beckoned me to sit with him on a big flat stone jutting from the corrie floor.

'Rest your bones,' he told me. 'There is more hunting to come.'

It was pleasant to sit there feeling the gradual quietening of the pulse of blood through my hard-used muscles. With closed eyes I lay back against another rock that backed on to our seat and relished the feeling, and when the throbbing and aching had died away I opened my eyes again and watched idly while the huntsmen went on with the work of gralloching.

I had enjoyed the hunt so far. I felt grateful to Alasdair for arranging to include me in it and I passed some such remark to him. He turned and studied me then with an intentness I found disconcerting.

'It was not solely for your pleasure I brought you with us today,' he said eventually. 'I wanted also an opportunity to speak with you where we would not be overheard, nor even overlooked, in private conversation.'

Surprised, I asked, 'But why? Is what you have to say so secret?'

Alasdair did not answer for a moment and then he said abruptly, 'Robert, I do not trust Captain Campbell of Glenlyon.'

I was quite taken aback at this unexpected declaration, and with anger flaring up inside me at his words I said stiffly, 'I am sorry you have thought it worth while to go to all this trouble for the opportunity to tell me so. However, I beg you to excuse me. I cannot discuss my superior officer with you.'

I rose to my feet as I finished speaking but he gripped the end of my plaid and pleaded. 'Wait! I beg you wait and hear me!'

'I have said already,' I told him coldly, 'I cannot discuss Glenlyon with you.'

'Then do not,' he urged, 'but listen to me, I beg you. I have something to tell you that will explain my reasons for speaking so.'

He was very much in earnest. I hesitated, looking at the pleading expression on his face, and at last I yielded ungraciously, 'Very well. I will listen.'

He sighed with relief and said, 'Sit down, then. 'Tis a long story.'

I took my place again on the rock and Alasdair began, 'It is a tale that has its roots in the time two years ago when the forces of King William were engaged in putting down the rebellion raised by those who remained loyal to James the Second after he had been deposed from the throne. My clan was out on the side of the rebels then, as you know. My father was at the head of our fighting-men and we were among those who defeated the Government forces in 1689 at the Battle of Killiecrankie.'

Now he had my interest in spite of myself for I could never resist any talk of military matters, and I had heard much of the famous charge of the clans which had routed the Government army at Killiecrankie.

'Were *you* there?' I asked.

Alasdair nodded. 'I was on my father's left and my brother John was on his right when he led our clan in the charge. We were on a rise of ground above the Government troops and we went down it like a storm breaking, the roar of our battle-cries the thunder of it and the flashing of our swords the lightning!'

I listened to him, wishing that I had been there myself to see that legendary charge and the massive old warrior, MacIan, pounding down the hill with his broadsword raised high and his sons pacing him on either side.

Alasdair smiled slightly at the expression on my face and added drily: 'Aye, it was a great victory for the clans. And we of Glencoe celebrated it as clans have celebrated victory in the Highlands from time immemorial. We took a creagh of our enemies' cattle on the road home from the battle.'

'A creagh?'

'A creagh is a lifting of cattle from a defeated enemy,' Alasdair explained, 'and on that occasion the cattle we took were those of Clan Campbell – that clan being on the Government side as well as being the traditional enemy of Clan Donald. We marched home through Campbell country on our road back to Glencoe, and as we marched we raided mightily among the cattle of the Earl of Breadalbane and those of Campbell of Glenlyon.'

'But that was—'

'Stealing?' He took the word out of my mouth and laughed grimly. 'There you are wrong! It is a recognized custom in the Highlands to raid the cattle of a defeated enemy. That is the way the clans have always warred and no Chief is considered any less a gentleman for carrying out a custom so honoured by time.'

He glanced sharply at me. 'Do you remember I told you that Breadalbane called my father "thief"?'

'Yes, when you spoke about my cousin marrying Breadalbane's kinsman. I remember.'

'It was that creagh that was the reason for the quarrel in which the insult was passed,' Alasdair said, 'and it was only the restraint of his fellow-Chiefs at the meeting where they quarrelled that prevented my father from killing Breadalbane. They parted in anger and Breadalbane swore to be avenged on the men of Glencoe.'

'But Glenlyon –' I asked, '– what had the quarrel to do with him?'

'It had this,' Alasdair said slowly. 'Glenlyon was born to a good inheritance but he had drunk and gambled most of it away before the time of Killiecrankie My father's raid on the Campbell cattle beggared him still further, and since then he has had only his Captain's pay to depend on – and whatever he can win out of Breadalbane.'

He looked inquiringly at me. 'Do you know the bye-name the clans have for Glenlyon?'

I shook my head and Alasdair said scornfully. 'They call him "Breadalbane's gillie" – and that is all he is. A servant for Breadalbane, a lackey to run before him to do his bidding – a menial to perform the tasks that would soil the Earl's own hands!'

Breathing hard from this invective he looked away northwards down the corrie towards the snow-caps of the mountains glistening white against the sky. With his eyes still turned towards them he said in a flat, quiet voice. 'That is why I do not trust Glenlyon – and why I fear his presence now in Glencoe.'

'MacIan does not fear him,' I said. 'He does not seem to have any doubts.'

Alasdair turned to look at me again. 'Glenlyon has eaten our salt. My father is an honourable man and that is sufficient proof for him that no treachery is intended.'

The anger I had swallowed rose sharply up in me again. 'It should be sufficient for you also–' I began, but Alasdair interrupted vehemently

'No, it is not! Glenlyon is a cunning man who sheds honour as easily when it suits him as I would toss a plaid over my shoulder! He runs like a dog before Breadalbane to do his bidding, and I do not believe that either of them could easily swallow the bitter feelings they have against us. Therefore, I do not believe in the reason Glenlyon gives for being in Glencoe now.'

He gripped my arm and swung me round to face him. 'Tell me, Robert, why are there Government troops in Glencoe? What are your *real* plans?'

'You have nothing to fear from us,' I told him. 'Our orders are–'

I checked abruptly then, horrified at what I had been about to say despite the instruction Glenlyon had given us the night before we left the Fort. '*Let no word of the action proposed against Glengarry escape you while we are in Glencoe.*' That had been his command, and he had added the warning, '*If the Glencoe men get the least wind of our intention they will put their Glengarry cousins on the qui vive.'* Yet here was I on the very verge of revealing our plans to a son of the Chief of the Glencoe Macdonalds!

Alasdair's voice broke urgently into the silence between us. 'Tell me, Robert! Tell me for friendship's sake. The Stewarts of Appin have always been good friends of the Macdonalds of Glencoe.'

His face was quite close to mine. I drew slowly back from it as he spoke for now I was seeing it as the face of a stranger – a stranger who might also be my enemy. The sweat of the hunt turned suddenly cold on my skin and I shivered.

Why should Alasdair, a man nearly nine years my senior in age, have shown so many marks of friendship towards me? Was it only because his wife was also a Stewart of Appin? Or was it because he thought that, being the youngest officer in Glenlyon's troop, I was the one most likely to give away our military secrets! Did he suspect that those secrets included an expedition against the Macdonells of Glengarry?

The branches of Clan Donald were all sworn by bonds of blood to stand by one another, and this watchful face staring at me now was a Clan Donald face Those dark eyes probing into mine were Clan Donald eyes. This voice appealing now to the bonds of friendship between Stewart and Macdonald could be the voice of a spy on the armed forces of the Crown!

I drew back sharply from him. I had thought this man my friend, but now I was seeing him as utterly alien to me. More than that, for he would not be trying to tease military information from me now unless he *was*, in fact, my enemy!

It was unthinkable for me to remain any longer in his company. The hunt was over, for me at least, that day. I rose to my feet. Between the sense of outrage I felt and the cold of dried sweat on my body I was shaking like someone in the grip of an ague, but I had something to say to this man and I forced myself to say it calmly, giving him the due formality of his full Gaelic title.

'I have told you, Alasdair Og MacIan, that your people have nothing to fear from our presence in the glen. More than that I cannot say without breaking my sworn oath of loyalty to the King. And this, if you are aware of honour at all, you must have known well before you began this conversation with me.'

With a curt word of farewell I turned on my heel. Alasdair sprang up after me and cried tauntingly. 'They will say you weakened and could not stand the pace if you do not stay for the rest of the hunt!'

'I had rather be taken for a weakling than know myself a knave!' I flung back over my shoulder at him, and walked on down the glen nursing my wrath like a wound.

As I trudged on I thanked Heaven for the French part of my heritage and for my upbringing abroad far from the clan squabbles of the Scottish Highlands At least, I thought grimly, these had given me a broader concept of honour than Alasdair Og MacIan who had tried to trade friendship for the sake of gaining fancied advantage over an enemy! And bitterly I wondered to myself how much of the story of the famous creagh was true and how much of it had been invented for the purpose of leading me to betray my senior officer's instructions.

It was a long walk back to Glencoe. I was exhausted by the time I reached my billet at Inverrigan, but once I had stripped off my Highland garb and donned my uniform again I came into a new lease of life. I felt at home again among my fellow officers and I thought that the cheerful red of their uniforms was the friendliest sight I had ever seen.

Glenlyon teased me over leaving the hunt early but I submitted to his jesting with a good grace, and as I took my place at table with him and the others I thought I had never been so glad to be back among my own kind again.

The talk over supper was of Flanders, of the part of the campaign there that was past and of the part yet to come when we would see active service, and Glenlyon led the conversation so well that even the taciturn Lindsay contributed his share of the discussion and Lundie was less dull than usual.

I talked and listened, completely absorbed in the military atmosphere I loved so well, and it was only once when Glenlyon used the phrase 'brothers-in-arms' that my mind flashed back to the scene of the hunt with Alasdair.

For a moment then I thought briefly and vividly of the

young huntsman laying my hand on his heart and calling me 'brother', and I remembered the feeling of pleasure this swearing of kinship had given me. Quickly I pushed the remembrance from me. The Army was my home and my true kinship was with the soldiers who served in it with me.

And remembering Alasdair's probing eyes and alien, watchful face I told myself grimly that if I did not wish to risk the taint of rebel on myself I would do well to remember these facts for the rest of our stay in Glencoe.

6 – And a mad soldier

There was a storm blowing up. I came to the door of my billet the next morning and saw the brow of it looking blackly over the mountain-walls that closed in the glen. The temperature had dropped sharply also and as we took breakfast Inverrigan prophesied snow before nightfall.

The Company officers had been invited to take a morning draught with the Chief's sons at John's house in Carnoch but I excused myself from going there with them for I had no inclination to meet face to face with Alasdair so soon after our quarrel. Instead, I thought, I would write a letter to my cousin Elizabeth and find a runner to take it to Glen Creran by way of the side-glen off Glen Muidhe which Alasdair had pointed out to me the previous day.

I sat down to my letter but found that the writing of it came hard after I had completed the first page. Apart from my hunting expedition and the hospitality we had received it seemed to me that there was little to recount of the eleven days we had spent in Glencoe. It had all been routine with not even the tax-gathering expeditions Glenlyon had hinted at to diversify the day's round for us.

I looked at the date I had written at the top of the page – 12th of February, 1692, and thought to myself that this would be just such another day as the eleven which had preceded it. Except that there would be snow before nightfall! Sighing, I crumpled the letter up and threw it into the fire. If that was all I had to write it was not worth sending.

There were no sports arranged for that day. There was not even a drill-parade to break the monotony, and for the rest of the morning I remained at Inverrigan feeling bored and discontented. I longed for some task to occupy me and when Glenlyon announced early in the afternoon that he was sending me with half the Company on a route-march to Ballachulish, I accepted the assignment eagerly. It was eight miles to Ballachulish and back and a route-march of that length would suit well to occupy me till suppertime!

'You will find Major Duncanson at the ferry inn at Ball-achulish,' Glenlyon told me after he had given me my first instructions. 'Report to him there and he will give you sealed orders for me.'

'Action, sir – at last?'

Glenlyon nodded, smiling his sleepy-lidded cat's smile at my eager question. 'Action,' he confirmed 'At last!'

In a totally different mood now I quickly mustered the troops he had directed me to take. Barbour was allotted to me as my Sergeant and we set off down the glen. The cold air numbed us at first, but a brisk marching pace brought the blood tingling back into our feet and the men swung along cheerfully with snatches of song breaking out here and there among them. I almost sang myself when I heard them strike up, and when Barbour turned on them and ordered them curtly to hold their tongues I, as curtly, countermanded his order. The dark glint of his eyes flashed bleak disapproval at me for a moment and then his face became its usual dour, impassive mask.

There was a surprise awaiting us at Ballachulish. We saw it from far off for there is nothing more conspicuous against a background of mountains than eight hundred men in red uniform coats. I glanced from the sight of them to look my amazement at Sergeant Barbour.

'What do you make of this, then, Sergeant?' I asked, and received stiffly in reply:

'I couldna say, sir.'

His tone, more than his words, told me clearly his poor opinion of junior officers who asserted themselves over Senior Sergeants, and much regretting the olive-branch I had offered him I withdrew into silence.

We marched on towards the ferry inn. There was great activity going on there with orderlies coming and going and boatloads of soldiers disembarking at the jetty to join the troops already camped out in all directions round the inn. I left Barbour in charge of our half-Company and made my way there.

'Ensign Stewart of Captain Campbell of Glenlyon's

Company reporting to Major Duncanson,' I told the sentry on duty at the door.

He passed me through and I knocked on the door of the inn-parlour. Duncanson was seated at the table inside the room with Captain Drummond standing beside his chair. As I came in Duncanson was saying:

'Those are Lieutenant Colonel Hamilton's orders, then, Captain. And you are to have a particular care that all ferry-boats are secured under guard before nightfall on the north side of the ferry.'

'Very good, sir. I will see it done,' Drummond answered.

He passed me on his way to the door and Duncanson called after him, 'Oh – and Captain Drummond! Send an orderly over to the north side of the ferry to tell Lieutenant Colonel Hamilton that Glenlyon's officer has reported for orders.'

'Very good, sir.'

Drummond went out and left me waiting for Duncanson to speak to me. The Major rummaged among the pile of papers on the table and picked out from among them a sealed letter.

'Here is a letter with orders in it for your Captain,' he said holding it out to me. 'Be sure to deliver it safely.'

I took it from him, longing but not daring to ask what the orders were. If it had been Major Forbes I would have risked the question but Major Duncanson was the most severe disciplinarian in the Fort and no junior officer like myself could expect anything but the strictest protocol from him. I waited to be dismissed but apparently the Major was not yet finished with me.

'Your Company is well distributed throughout Glencoe?' he asked.

'Oh yes, sir,' I assured him. 'We have shared the burden of billeting very fairly among the people.'

'And the Macdonalds are friendly towards you?'

'Yes, sir, we are on the best of terms with them, I would say.'

'The men are in good spirits?'

'Yes, sir. They keep very cheerful.'

75

'And good discipline has been maintained — their training has not been allowed to lapse?'

'Yes, sir. Sergeant Barbour has seen to that.'

'Ah, yes, Sergeant Barbour. He is with you today, is he not?'

'Yes, sir.'

'Very good, Ensign. I will have a word with the Sergeant before you return to Glencoe You may dismiss.'

I saluted and left the inn. The Sergeant had the men drawn neatly up by the boat-slip. I sent him off to see Major Duncanson and stood watching the next boatful of soldiers arriving while I waited for him to return.

There was a familiar figure standing up in the bow of the incoming boat. As it grounded I hailed him.

'Francis! Hey, Francis!'

Francis Farquhar looked round at my hail, then leapt from the boat to hurry up the jetty.

'What's afoot, Francis?' I greeted him. 'There are nearly four hundred troops here on this side of the ferry and you seem to have as many more drawn up on the opposite bank. What's in the wind?'

'Have *you* had no orders?' he countered.

'Not yet,' I told him, 'but I have just now got a sealed letter from Major Duncanson with orders in it for Glenlyon.'

He sighed and turned away from me to look out glumly over the loch. 'I know no more than you do then about all this activity. The rumour is that we are going out at last against Glengarry but—'

I waited for him to continue and when he did not speak I pressed him, 'But what?'

He made no reply for a moment, then slowly he said, 'Major Forbes is Lieutenant Colonel Hamilton's second-in-command for the detachment of Hill's Regiment over there on the other side of the loch, but *he* is not happy with the orders he has been given! Some of us have overheard him quarrelling with Hamilton — indeed, he has been shouting so with rage that we could not help overhearing him!'

He turned full face to me again. 'Forbes told Hamilton that he was unfit to be an officer He called him an underhanded schemer and a lick-spittle. Then he shouted, *"My sword is bound to your command but you shall not have my honour! I shall resign my commission before I allow you to take that from me also!"'*

Shocked, I exclaimed, 'Forbes would never resign from the Service! He is a soldier born and bred, Francis – why *should* he make such a threat! And what could he hope to achieve with it, in any case?'

'Scandal,' Francis answered briefly. 'He could force an inquiry into the reasons for his resignation and thus bring to public knowledge whatever operation it is that Hamilton is planning for the troops here today.'

I glanced round at the soldiers milling about the jetty and at those on the opposite bank of the loch. 'There must be nearly the whole garrison of Fort William here, Francis,' I protested, 'and Hamilton could not have brought all these men out without orders from high authority. Are you sure Forbes was not simply out of temper because no one had consulted him in the planning of the operation?'

'I am positive!' Francis said vehemently. 'Forbes does have a fiery temper, I agree, but his nature is a just and generous one. He would not have spoken so to Hamilton out of petty spite.'

I caught sight of Sergeant Barbour at that moment, emerging from the door of the inn.

'I will have to go now,' I told Francis. 'There is my Sergeant coming – but tell me quickly first. Have you had any further word from Elizabeth?'

'Yes, but the position is still the same,' he said dispiritedly.'Your great-aunt is determined on this fine marriage for her.'

And that was probably the reason for half his forebodings, I thought to myself as I took my leave of him and rejoined my men. He was so low in spirits over Elizabeth that he was taking the gloomiest view of everything else as well – including the quarrel between Major Forbes and Lieutenant Colonel Hamilton.

It was a regrettable thing, of course, yet there were bound to be disagreements on military tactics sometimes among the higher ranks. Why should that concern us junior officers? We could not influence our seniors' decisions, after all, and we would have to fight just the same whatever form the campaign took.

What *were* the orders I carried? My hand rose to touch the place where they rested snugly inside my coat and the paper crackled slightly at the movement. Whatever they were, I thought, they spelt action at last, and felt my heart begin to race fast at the excitement of the prospect. Our marching pace seemed too slow for me. I could hardly wait to get back to Glencoe, and besides, the afternoon sky was already darkening over and the east wind cutting into our faces was whirling with it the first flakes of the snow Inverrigan had prophesied would come before nightfall.

'Increase your marching rate by ten paces to the minute,' I told Sergeant Barbour. 'There is snow in that wind.'

'Very good, sir.' Barbour quickened the pace, calling out the beat to the men and, heads down against the ever-increasing force of the wind, we marched on at our altered pace.

For another hour the snow held off then gradually it began to drive more thickly past us. The flakes were the small stinging kind that felt like handfuls of salt being thrown against the face. I pulled the collar of my coat as high as it would go and sent Barbour to the rear to keep any stragglers up with the main body while I continued to set the pace myself from in front of the ranks.

Like this we re-entered Glencoe. It was full dark by that time and the lit windows of the glen's little houses were welcome beacons to us. Sergeant Barbour, I knew, would have a report to make to Glenlyon on his interview with Major Duncanson, and so I dismissed the various troops in charge of their Corporals while Barbour and I continued together to the house of the tacksman, Inverrigan.

There was a full company gathered inside it. As Barbour and I stood at the door stamping the snow off our boots I noted John and Alasdair playing cards with Glenlyon and a neighbour of Inverrigan's. Lundie and Lindsay were looking on at the game while Inverrigan himself and his wife sat by the fire in conversation with some other neighbours of theirs.

Everyone looked up as we came in and there were exclamations at the way the blizzard was blowing up. Glenlyon rose and came towards me saying, 'Well?' with his hand outstretched for the orders. I glanced doubtfully at the curious faces watching us but Glenlyon said impatiently, 'Give it here, Ensign.'

I drew the paper from my coat and handed it to him. Quickly he broke the seal from it and scanned what was written there. His face was ruddy from the warmth of the room, but as he read the blood drained out of it and the network of veins left standing out against its paleness gave it the mottled look of marble. His back was to the rest of the company so that no one but myself and Barbour saw the blood leave his face, and by the time he had finished reading the flush had crept back into his cheeks. He re-folded the paper, a smile quirking his mouth, and when he turned to face the company again it was in his usual jovial tones that he cried out:

'My friends, I have news that will take me from this pleasant fireside!'

'Bad news?' Alasdair asked swiftly.

'No, no! Nothing of that sort.' He turned to me. 'Stewart, go clear the Corporal out of Number One guard-post. I will need it for an officer's conference. Meet me there.'

I turned to go and as I left the room I heard him cry, 'Now do not disturb yourselves from the fire, my friends. I must speak with my officers but we will not let that come between you and your evening's pleasure.'

I went quickly to the small guard-post nearby Inverrigan's house. Kennedy was the Corporal on duty that night. I gave him the order to clear the post for Glenlyon's use and to stand by for further orders, but instead of moving to the door he continued to stand to attention and gaze at me with an unhappy expression on his face.

'Move, Corporal!' I snapped at him 'The Captain will be here at any moment.'

Kennedy continued to stare unhappily at me. ' 'Tis MacEachern, sir, Private MacEachern,' he blurted out. 'I was waiting till you came back to tell you about him, sir. He said *"Tell Mr Stewart"* he said to me. *"Tell him the gale is above the heather*." He has been behaving very strangely, sir. I fear he is sick.'

I hesitated, torn between annoyance at this stupid story and concern for the trouble the fool, MacEachern, seemed to be in.

'Where is he?' I asked.

'He is only a few steps off from the post, sir,' Kennedy said eagerly. 'Will you see him, sir?'

'Oh, very well,' I agreed impatiently. 'But be quick, man.'

I led the way out of the guard-post. 'Over there, sir,' Kennedy pointed to a small group of houses twenty yards away and led the way towards them. Voices drifted to me out of the dark and swirling snow as I hurried after him and I recognized Glenlyon's tones among them. He was already on his way to the guard-post, I realized, and conscious of the rebuke that would be mine when he arrived and found I was not waiting there as ordered, I halted and snapped at Kennedy.

'I cannot spare you any more time for this nonsense, Corporal. Where is the man?'

'There, sir, leaning against the wall of that house. He said he would not put a roof over his head till he had spoken with you.'

I peered through swirling snow and Kennedy urged me on a few steps to the dark outline of the house he had pointed out. MacEachern was leaning against the wall, the back of his head pressed against it, his face upturned. Snow clung thickly to the front of his red uniform coat, his hair and beard were powdered with snow-flakes, and in the light from the window further along the wall the moisture from melted snow gleamed on his face. His eyes staring blindly out of his wet face were fixed on some private nightmare world of terror that contained neither myself nor Corporal Kennedy.

'He has stood staring like that for hours, sir,' Kennedy whispered.

Quite clearly, I decided, the man was in some sort of a trance and there was nothing for it but to bring him out of it as sharply as possible.

'He will not stay so much longer,' I retorted, and slapped MacEachern hard on one cheek. His head jerked with the blow. Slowly he raised one hand and felt his face and then looked at me with the light of recognition coming back into his eyes In a hoarse, slow voice he said, 'Sir – Mr Stewart, sir, I have had a vision.'

I almost shouted with exasperation. Here was I called to an urgent conference of officers and this great silly fool was making me late with his babbling about a vision.

'Get back to the guard-post, Corporal,' I said furiously. 'I will soon deal with this!'

The Corporal made off to the guard-post as I turned back to MacEachern. 'Now listen to me, MacEachern—' I began, but he broke into my words,

'No, no, Mr Stewart, sir, you must listen to *me* for it was a terrible vision I saw, and before God, sir, I swear it will all come true for I am cursed with the second-sight and all the men of my family before me—'

I brushed away his hands clutching at me and tried to stem the spate of his words babbling on but he continued, not heeding me, his eyes bulging with terror and distress.

'—I saw blood, sir, much blood, and it was spilt on the snow. I saw the rocks sticking through the snow run red with the blood. I saw a baby's hand severed from its body lying in the snow, and a boy – just a wee lad he was, with a dirk piercing his throat. I saw men shot and stabbed and falling, falling one after the other with wide-open eyes and tossing arms. I saw the gale above the heather, sir, and I knew it was Macdonald men that were falling . . .'

His voice rose to a hoarse shout 'Sir, sir, listen to me for you are the only one of them I can trust – the only one of them that is not a Campbell! I saw the gale above the heather . . . There is danger to Glencoe, sir! The gale is above the heather . . .'

I gripped him by the shoulders and shook him as hard as I could. It was not just a simpleton I had to deal with now, I realized. The man was mad. There was no doubt in my mind about that. It was urgent that I should calm him and the best way to do so would be to appear to believe in his delusions.

'You must tell MacIan about this!' I shouted in his ear.

MacEachern's babbling stopped abruptly. 'MacIan . . .?' he repeated, staring at me.

I seized the opportunity of the moment to talk as rapidly and convincingly as I could.

' 'Tis a wonderful vision you have had, Private MacEachern, but surely if there is danger threatening Glencoe it is MacIan, the Chief, you must tell. He has the right to know, has he not?'

He nodded, but his eyes were still wide with fear. 'A Chief is a great man, sir,' he mumbled. 'He would not be listening to a poor clansman like me.'

'Then you must tell Alasdair Og MacIan,' I hurried on, improvising wildly. 'He is a good young man and very close in his heart to the men of the clan. He will listen to you.'

'I will go now,' MacEachern decided instantly. He tried to move away from me but I had no intention of letting this madman loose to run about spreading alarm through the glen. I held him fast, wishing I had not been so hasty in dismissing the Corporal and casting around in my mind for some way of dealing with MacEachern on my own.

'Wait! Wait, MacEachern!' I cried, 'or your haste may spoil matters Danger must be met with cunning, after all, and you do not even know yet what day your vision will come true!'

He stared unhappily at me. 'Aye,' he muttered. 'Aye. It has happened that way before.'

I had him now! So long as he was doubtful of anything about his vision he would listen to my persuasions. And I had to persuade him if I was to keep him under control long enough to have him safely locked away. I released my grip on him and stepped back.

'Listen closely, then, Private MacEachern,' I said in my best voice of command, 'and I will tell you what to do. You will mention this vision to no one else but me, and you will go quietly to your quarters. There you will wait till I send for you, and meanwhile, if anything happens to tell you that the danger in your vision is close at hand, you will run like a hare to warn Alasdair Og MacIan about it. That is an order. You understand?'

'Yes, sir!' He tried to come to attention and salute but he was frozen with standing so long in the cold and moved as clumsily as a bear. However, the mere attempt at the gesture showed that his mind was coming back to normal, and a little sigh of relief escaped me at the thought. I kept up the charade I was playing with him by returning the salute and barking, '*Dis-miss!*' at him.

He faced about and marched clumsily off in the direction of his billet. I let him take a few steps away from me and then turned and ran as hard as I could back to the guard-post. The man's condition would have to be reported immediately to Glenlyon so that he could either be put under restraint or – if he continued in the quiet mood I had induced in him – put on the sick list.

The guard-post door was shut. Corporal Kennedy, who should have been standing sentry in front of it, was sheltering from the driving snow behind the lee wall of the building. I thrust open the door, and with the snow still stinging in my eyes, blundered across the threshold. Glenlyon's voice came to me, topping the wave of voices and laughter that met me as I entered.

'. . . and the gale will be above the heather!'

I stood gaping stupidly at him. '*What* was that you said, sir?'

He walked towards me, grinning, and kicked the door shut behind me. The papers with the orders I had brought him dangled from the fingers of his right hand.

'I was remarking, Ensign Stewart, that before this night is over, the gale will be above the heather.'

His grin widened to a laugh at the baffled expression on my face. 'I see I will have to explain – I keep forgetting you are not Highland bred for all you are a Stewart of Eilidh,' he remarked. 'The little plant called "gale" or bog-myrtle, Ensign, is the badge of the Clan Campbell, and the heather is the badge of Clan Donald. And if you read these orders you will see the full meaning of that explanation.'

I took the paper he handed me and read the orders on it. For a long moment after I had finished reading I continued to stare unseeingly at the paper, for there was a memory between me and the crabbed handwriting of Major Duncanson. The memory was that of a bearded face with snow glistening on the cheek-bones and haunted eyes staring out of it. A voice echoed in my ears, the hoarse voice of Private MacEachern shouting.

'There is danger to Glencoe, sir! The gale is above the heather . . .'

And dazedly I thought, 'He was *not* mad – dear God, *he was not mad at all!*'

7 'You are hereby ordered—'

The order-paper was headed with the date 12th February, 1692, and it read,

You are hereby ordered to fall upon the rebels, the Macdonalds of Glencoe, and put all to the sword under seventy. You are to have special care that the old fox and his sons do not escape your hands; you are to secure all avenues that no man escape. This you are to put into execution at five of the clock precisely; and by that time, or very shortly after it, I will strive to be at you with a stronger party. If I do not come to you at five, you are not to tarry for me, but to fall on. This is by the King's special commands, for the good and safety of the country, that these miscreants be cut off root and branch. See that this be put into execution without fear or favour, or you may expect to be dealt with as one not true to King or Government, nor a man fit to carry a commission in the King's service. Expecting you will not fail in the fulfilling hereof, as you love yourself. I subscribe this at Ballachulish, the 12th of February, 1692.

Robert Duncanson

The instructions were clear. The enormity of the treachery involved in them was impossible to grasp. The shock they conveyed through my whole body set the paper trembling in my hands. Glenlyon took it from me and said,

'We have all had the opportunity to read the orders now. I will give out the assignments.'

I found my voice then and cried, 'Sir! We cannot do this! It would be murder to fall thus upon men who have been our hosts!'

Glenlyon surveyed me slowly up and down and in a voice that had an edge like a knife to it he remarked, 'I thought I would have trouble with you!'

He turned to the others standing silently watching us. 'Barbour,' he commanded, 'get you to Achnacon. Lundie, you take Carnoch and you, Lindsay, take Inverrigan. Draw the men by batches to the guard-houses at each place and tell them what to do. At five of the clock precisely they are to rise and carry out the instructions in Major Duncanson's letter. Tell them to use cold steel only. Musket shots would raise the alarm and allow some to escape. When all the men have been given their orders, double the number of guards on duty and give orders for the guard to be changed every hour. When you have finished, all three of you, report back to me here.'

The three men tramped out. I could not believe what was happening – I could not credit the evidence of my own eyes and ears. My mind willed my voice to protest, my body to block their way, but nothing happened. I stayed voiceless and rooted to the spot with the numbing horror of it all.

I thought Glenlyon must have been drinking again. On the table stood cups and a flask of wine he must have brought over with him from Inverrigan's house, but he made no move to pour wine for himself when the other three had left and when he turned to me I saw that I had guessed wrongly. His face was flushed and his eyes glittered with a strange, elated look, but he was sober.

'Sit down!' he commanded.

I shook my head. 'No!' I croaked, and then more strongly, '*No!*' Full power of speech came flooding back to me.

'You cannot do this thing, Glenlyon,' I shouted. 'You cannot murder men who have given you bed and board and friendship for two weeks! Not the lowest churl, the meanest thief could stoop so low!'

'I have my orders—' he began, and I interrupted him.

'Orders! No soldier is called on to obey an order to murder!' I glared at him, choking with the strength of my emotions. 'Murderer,' I shouted. 'You are no soldier and no gentleman, Glenlyon, you are a common murderer!'

He took one swift step that brought him towering over me. The flat of his hand cracked sharply against my cheek and while I still reeled from the blow he raged at me:

'You think I have no cause to wish the Glencoe Macdonalds dead, eh? You think I have no just reason for wishing revenge on them! Well, listen to me, my fine young cock-alorum, and I will tell you what I have to revenge. MacIan and his sons beggared me. Two years ago they took a creagh of cattle off my lands – two thousand pounds worth of black cattle they stole, and they have laughed at me over it ever since. They and the whole of Clan Donald have laughed at me. But a Macdonald does not laugh long at a Campbell, and this night I will slit the laugh out of their bellies and leave them hawk's meat in the morning!'

So Alasdair had told me truly about the creagh!

I crouched where I had fallen against the table, staring up at him. His tall form was bent over me, long hair falling forward on either side of his flushed face. His eyes were glittering at me with a maniac's rage. I straightened up, holding his gaze with my own and asked quietly:

'Who planned such sweet revenge for you – the Earl of Breadalbane?'

Glenlyon's wide, fanatic gaze narrowed in suspicion. 'Who told you that?'

'That is an admission in itself!' I exclaimed. 'It *was* Breadalbane who planned this massacre!'

His mouth opened as if for angry denial of my accusation and then, as though suddenly deeming this hardly worth while in the circumstances, he said casually:

'Since you seem to know so much of the affair already – yes, it was!'

'But how?' I stared at him in perplexity. 'Breadalbane does not rule Scotland.'

'Never mind how it was done.' He smiled his sleepy cat's smile at me. 'My Lord Breadalbane knows many ways to pull the strings of power!'

I looked him up and down and with all the scorn I could muster in my eyes and voice I jeered at him, *'Breadalbane's gillie!'* Glenlyon seized me to himself, holding me with both hands clenched in the stuff of my coat. Hissing at me, his face so close to my own that his spittle fell on me, he choked out,

'One more such word from you, and before God, I'll drive a dirk through your heart!'

Slowly he loosed his hold on me. We backed a step or two from one another, both panting with the rage and exertion of the moment. Our eyes held for a few seconds more and then in a quieter voice I said:

'You will not succeed, Glenlyon, even though you take the

Macdonalds by surprise. There are only a hundred and twenty of us – not enough even in these circumstances to wipe out a clan of some five hundred souls.'

Glenlyon laughed. 'I know more of these people's ways than you do! MacIan was not sure at first whether we came as friends or foes, and so the first thing he would do would be to order all his fighting-men to hide their weapons in case we arrested them as armed rebels. You can depend on it that all their swords and dirks have been so safely hidden these past twelve days that they will not be easy to get at in a hurry.

'And as to comparative numbers – why do you think there were all these troops at Ballachulish? Duncanson will arrive at Carnoch at five o'clock with another four hundred men to block the western exit from the glen. Lieutenant Colonel Hamilton will bring as many more by way of Kinlochleven and over the Devil's Staircase to the eastern end of the glen. Eight hundred men to net the glen for us, my lad, and help us forward with the work – and none of them as weak-kneed over it as you are!'

'Call me what you like,' I retorted angrily, 'you will not get me to join in your filthy scheme for revenge!'

'No?' he queried satirically. 'No?' He lifted the order-paper and read from it:

See that this be put into execution without fear or favour, or you may expect to be dealt with as one not true to King or Government, nor a man fit to carry a commission in the King's service. Expecting you will not fail in this, as you love yourself . . .'

He glanced over the paper to me. 'You hear that? "–as you love yourself . . ." That is Duncanson's pleasant way of telling me that I will be court-martialled if I disobey this order As you will be, Ensign Stewart. As you will be—'

He folded the paper and tossed it down on the table. 'Major Duncanson seems to have feared that my fortnight's stay in Glencoe has softened me towards the Macdonalds, but he need not have troubled! I am still as hot against them as I was when Hamilton first proposed his scheme for tricking them into accepting us as harmless. The plan still sorts as well with my private schemes of revenge. But even if it did not, I would still carry it out. For I *do* love myself, Ensign Stewart. I do not wish to be court-martialled, stripped of my rank, shot. Do you?'

'No, but – I – I—'

'You are set on a career in the Army,' Glenlyon pressed remorselessly on over my stammering, 'and young as you are, I will say this for you, that you are a born soldier. Carry out this order as you would any other and, whatever you may think of it personally, no blame will attach to you. But refuse this order and you will have violated the oath of loyalty you swore to the King when you were commissioned – especially so because, as it states here – *this is by the King's special commands.*'

He tapped the order with his forefinger on these last words and paused, his face inviting me to speak. I sank down on a stool beside the table and rested my head in my hands. Glenlyon's words were all true, horribly true. What faced me now was a choice between joining in a plot to murder some hundreds of unsuspecting people who had shown me nothing but friendship, or of blasting all the hopes for myself that I held most dear.

Despair gripped me. I looked up at Glenlyon and saw that he was regarding me now with a kindly, almost paternal air.

'Stewart,' he said, 'forget for a moment my personal stake in the matter and look at it simply as a military manoeuvre. Glengarry is in defiance of the Government and the other rebel Chiefs took the oath with reluctance. We have not the time to subdue Glengarry by force before we are needed in Flanders, yet cannot risk those other Chiefs following his example as soon as we are out of the country. Therefore it has been decided to treat with Glengarry while we take one small clan – the Macdonalds of Glencoe – and make such an example of it as will frighten all the other Chiefs out of any notion of rebellion. Our talk of going out against Glengarry was only a blind to screen this purpose, which had to be achieved secretly or not at all since Glencoe is such a good natural stronghold for the Macdonalds. Do you understand?'

Wearily I told him, 'Of course I understand. It is the treachery of making the Macdonalds our hosts and then turning on them that I cannot swallow.'

'It is the only way to ensure their complete destruction.' Grim once again, Glenlyon stared down at me. 'So you had better swallow it or you, too, will be hawk's meat by the morning!'

He drew his pistol and cocked the hammer. Pointing the weapon at my head he leaned forward quickly and whipped my pistol from my belt.

'And now,' he commanded, 'your sword!'

Slowly, my fingers fumbling on the buckles, I unfastened the belt that held my father's sword and handed it to him He sat down at the table opposite me and carefully laid the belt and the pistol on the floor beside him.

'Now, Stewart,' he said, 'you have read Duncanson's warning to me. I am a beggared man since MacIan robbed me. My Captain's commission is all I have left and I do not intend to let you endanger that also. I will give you time to decide whether your are for me or against me, but decide you must. Or die.'

'I understand,' I told him dully, and then rested my head on my hands again and tried to think.

If I accepted the order to murder the Macdonalds I would have nothing but my own conscience to accuse me. If I refused the order, Glenlyon would shoot me. That was the choice he had laid before me – yet there was still another alternative. I could try to escape from the guard-house and warn the Macdonalds of the impending massacre.

I might still be shot while trying to do this, of course, but Glenlyon himself had pointed out that the sound of fire-arms would disturb the glen and alert the victims to their fate. The thought of that might make him hesitate long enough in his shot to let me break free. I would stand some chance of success if I took this third course

And yet, I thought despairingly, it would just as certainly put an end to my career in the Army as if I had died at Glenlyon's hands. I would be a fugitive afterwards – a deserter guilty of high treason. I would never fight in the King's Army again.

Why, oh why had I not foreseen what was about to happen! There had been plenty of signs to warn me, from the discovery of Hamilton's secret correspondence onwards. I should have linked Francis Farquhar's suspicions of this with other things, I thought. And in bitter self-reproach I recalled these things, one by one.

There was Hamilton's hint that he knew of matters which were being kept from Major Forbes; the contrast between Glenlyon's polite good-humour when we dined with MacIan on our first night in the glen and his derisive whisper afterwards about 'the old fox and his cubs' – his frequent talks in secret with Barbour and the strangely aloof attitude of Lundie and Lindsay. There was Alasdair's story about the creagh and his warnings about the connection between Glenlyon and Breadalbane and – that very day – the way Duncanson had established with his questions to me how the suspicons of the Macdonalds had been lulled, and how well placed we were to take them by surprise!

Separately these things meant nothing – but I should have been alert enough to connect them with one another and to realize that they added up to treachery of some kind. Why, Glenlyon himself had practically told me what that treachery was when he laughed so excessively at the story of the too-trusting giant who was killed in his sleep!

Fairly squirming with self-reproach now I thought, 'No wonder he laughed!' The story had been a perfect allegory of his own plan and the presence of Inverrigan – one of the very men marked for slaughter – must have added savour to my innocent telling of it. It must indeed have been marvellously amusing – to anyone who had the stomach for so black a jest!

I owed Alasdair Og MacIan an apology, I thought, and shuddered to think that Alasdair would be dead before daylight. I looked up and saw Glenlyon watching me intently.

'Well?' he asked.

'Give me time,' I muttered. 'Give me time to – to decide.'

Glenlyon scowled at my plea. 'You will be the first to die if you decide wrongly,' he warned. 'And I shall then be forced to record, with sorrow, that it was a bullet from the pistol of some fleeing Macdonald which killed you!'

He drew out his watch and placing it on the table between us, nodded to it. 'I will give you one hour from now to tell me yea or nay.'

The watch's hour hand pointed to ten. I had not thought so much time to have passed since I came back with the orders! I sat looking at the minute hand of the watch and was appalled at the way it seemed to be racing round the dial. I had to decide quickly what I was going to do.

I wanted to stay in the Army. I wanted it more than anything else on earth. I wanted to rise in rank as my father had done and to earn the same respect from my men and junior officers that he had always had. What would *he* have done in such a situation as this, I wondered. Would he have agreed that a soldier's oath of loyalty absolves him of responsibility for any action he is ordered to take? Or would he have put the law of conscience higher than his oath?

Desperately I tried to recall the sound of his voice but all I could hear was the wind's wild howling. I tried to picture his face but all I could see was the thin, sneering face of Glenlyon opposite me. With my hands over my eyes I shut out the sight of it and into the darkness behind my concealing palms flashed the memory of my father's honest, kindly face. And suddenly I knew beyond a doubt that if I consented to take part in the massacre I would be ashamed ever to recall that face to my memory again.

For the moment that this flash of understanding lasted I felt so elated that I wanted to laugh aloud, but cold realization of everything implied by my decision followed hard on the heels of the elated moment. I was throwing away my whole career, turning my back on the only thing I had ever wanted to do. I must plan it so that my gesture was not wasted. I must warn as many of the Macdonalds as I could before five o'clock the following morning.

I began to plan. First of all I must deceive Glenlyon on my intentions towards him. Then, when a chance came to make my break for freedom, I would have to rely on his reluctance to let the sound of shooting rouse the glen prematurely. How should I time my break and whom should I warn first?

The nearby houses of Inverrigan were out of the question. I

would be caught and brought down by shot or steel if I lingered to warn any of the people there. That left Achnacon and Carnoch as the two other main centres of population, and as soon as I thought of the possibility of warning Alasdair at Carnoch I remembered Private MacEachern.

I felt a cold grue run down my back then! In the Fort I had sneered at the idea of the 'second-sight' MacEachern was said to have. That very evening I had jumped to the conclusion that his simple mind had broken down into madness Now I had to acknowledge that this simple fellow did indeed have the strange gift that was said to be given to some Highlanders. He had seen into the future of Glencoe and his vision had indeed been a terrible one.

There was hope in the mere fact of it, however. MacEachern would be among those given their orders for the massacre by this time. He would know now for certain that his vision would come true that very night – and I had ordered him to run and tell Alasdair the minute he had reason to believe that this was the case!

The question now was whether he would be able to do so without being shot by his own comrades-in-arms. They were all Campbells. They would not allow one of their own number to betray them. MacEachern would realize this as soon as the orders were given out to his troop and he was not mad as I had thought. He was sane – quite sane enough to calculate that he would have to wait his opportunity to run to Carnoch and warn Alasdair.

But he would make the effort to go if he could. I was sure of that. He was of the Clan Donald blood and he had his vision to spur him on. Moreover, he had my order to back up his belief that he would be doing the proper thing in warning Alasdair. He trusted me – he had said himself that that was why he had told me of his vision. He had accepted the order I had given him and, I reasoned, the poor fellow would probably trust to that order of mine to save him from a firing-squad if he was caught giving the warning.

That left Achnacon for me to rouse. I calculated that even in the teeth of the blizzard I could reach Achnacon in just over half an hour, I would have to have time enough in hand to warn the inhabitants once I arrived there. Yet I could not afford to make my break too soon or Glenlyon might try to forestall my warning attempt by putting the whole time of the massacre forward. I would have to time it so that it was not worth his while to do that.

I stole another glance at the watch. Three minutes before eleven o'clock. I would time my break as near as possible to four o'clock. That meant that two out of the three main centres of population in the glen would stand some chance of being warned before five o'clock struck. It was the best I could do in the circumstances.

I took a deep breath. 'I have decided where my duty lies,' I told Glenlyon. 'I will obey the order.'

He looked up under his brows at me. I was not practiced in deceit and my glance wavered before his. Without a word he reached an arm to the flagon of wine, poured two cups from it and handed one to me. Quietly he said then:

'We will drink to that.'

He tossed his wine off in a single swallow. I set my own cup reluctantly to my lips, and as I did so Glenlyon said: 'I will keep your sword and pistol as surety for your good faith, however, and give them back to you at five o'clock.'

I took a mouthful of wine without answering him and was swallowing it down when he added, '—in order to let you kill our host, Inverrigan. Then I will be sure of you.'

I choked on the wine, coughing and spluttering while he watched me with a grim smile stretched tight on his features. Footsteps outside saved me from having to think of some reply to this. The door swung open to let Lieutenant Lindsay enter. He began making his report to Glenlyon and while he was speaking Ensign Lundie and Sergeant Barbour also returned to the guard-post. Glenlyon heard each of them out and when the last one was finished he asked:

'Was there any trouble among the men – any objections to the orders?'

The three men exchanged glances with one another. Lindsay spoke, hesitantly:

'There was some grumbling – not openly, of course, and not

against the prospect of killing Macdonalds. But I did overhear some complaints against the method chosen.'

'Lundie? Barbour?' Glenlyon glanced questioningly at each of the other two in turn, and each briefly confirmed what Lindsay had said. Lindsay added, 'There was one fellow – Private MacEachern, who seemed to be the ring-leader of the complaints at Number 3 Inverrigan guard-post. I had the Corporal there put him in close custody and warned him he would be put on a charge of mutiny.'

Glenlyon nodded. 'Very good, Lieutenant. That should teach the others a sharp lesson.'

He turned to Barbour. 'You return to Achnacon, Sergeant. Kill the tacksman and his relatives first, for without Achnacon himself to lead them the other men there will fall into confusion. And remember, use cold steel only.'

'Yes, sir!' Barbour came smartly to attention and saluted. With his black bullet-head and stiff figure he looked more like something made out of iron than a man of flesh and blood. Only his flinty little eyes seemed alive and they, I saw with renewed horror, were glittering now with an eager, expectant light. I had been right about this man! He killed for pleasure, and already in his mind he was enjoying the murder of Achnacon and his tenants.

Glenlyon poured wine for the other two officers after the departure of Barbour. He offered to re-fill my cup also but I shook my head. Lindsay asked, looking curiously at me:

'Is he with us, sir?'

'Yes, I have persuaded him it is not worth sacrificing himself for the sake of a few rebels. But he will bear watching yet, I think.'

Glenlyon grinned sardonically at me again. He drank his wine and the other two drank with him. Lundie put more peats on the fire and sat down beside it with Lindsay. Glenlyon kept his place opposite me at the table, and like this we sat for the next hour and a half.

The storm outside the guard-house still raged as wildly as ever and they discussed it from time to time.

Glenlyon said, 'That mountainous route over the Devil's

Staircase is a difficult one at the best of times. This blizzard means that Hamilton may arrive late at the eastern end of the glen.'

'Major Duncanson will arrive in good time to support us,' Lindsay said. 'He has only four miles to come from Ballachulish.'

I listened to them, wondering whether Francis Farquhar had been assigned to one of these two companies and, if this was the case, how he had received the orders for the massacre. Was he marching to the slaughter now, or was there any hope that he had rebelled as I had done?

Glenlyon's watch still lay on the table between us. At half past twelve there was a sound of voices raised outside the door of the guard-post – Corporal Kennedy's issuing the challenge and Alasdair's brusquely demanding to see the Captain.

'Cover Stewart!' Glenlyon said sharply to Lundie. 'If he so much as opens his mouth, shoot him. Shoot to kill!'

With a speed that surprised me Lundie swung his bulky form across the room and took up a stance close behind my stool. I felt the muzzle of a pistol pressed against my back and heard the click of the hammer as he cocked it. Glenlyon snatched up a satchel lying in a corner and shouted to the Corporal to let Alasdair pass. By the time the door opened he had pulled a map from the satchel and spread it out on the table. He and Lindsay were bent in apparent study of it, and with one hand on my shoulder and the other forcing the pistol against my spine, Lundie had pushed me forward and was holding me so that I also appeared to be part of the map-studying group.

Alasdair came in beating the snow from his shoulders and challenged Glenlyon immediately.

'What is all this stir then, Glenlyon? I have just now seen with my own eyes that the guards in all your posts are doubled, and there are too many of your men still awake for my liking.'

I strained upwards and saw him glowering angrily at Glenlyon. 'There is treachery afoot – Campbell treachery!' he shouted.

'Tch, tch, Alasdair,' Glenlyon reproved him mildly. 'I will

forgive you these words because your wife is kin to my wife and that ties bonds of friendship between us—'

'To the devil with your soft talk of kinship,' Alasdair roared. '*Your* blood is all Campbell! Why are you awake at this hour – you and your officers? What orders did you receive tonight from Ballachulish? What Campbell plot is brewing here in Glencoe?'

I could have shouted out to him. Only one word of warning was needed for as soon as it left my lips Lundie would shoot and my death would tell Alasdair all he needed to know. It would also be the signal for his own death, however. Glenlyon would never let him leave the guard-post alive with the knowledge the shot would give him. I knew I could accomplish nothing by dying then, and so I kept silent.

Glenlyon became suddenly dignified in the face of Alasdair's shouted questions. 'I go against my command in telling you this, Alasdair Og MacIan,' he said stiffly, 'but if nothing less will satisfy you I will tell you that there are orders gone out against Macdonell of Glengarry, and those were the ones I received this evening. I am holding my troops in readiness to march with the rest of the regiment for this purpose, and as you can see, my officers are presently studying the terrain over which we may have to fight.'

He gestured to the map on the table. Lindsay looked up from it with a polite and puzzled expression on his face, and both he and Lundie murmured agreement with Glenlyon. I tried desperately to catch Alasdair's eye so that I could signal some sort of message to him but he glanced away from me, my quarrel with him still showing in the hostile look that skimmed past my face.

'Have you discussed this with MacIan?' Glenlyon asked suavely. 'It is surely his place, after all, to challenge my intentions.'

'I have spoken to him.' The admission was dragged out of Alasdair.

'And what did he say?'

Alasdair was not nearly so certain of himself now. Sullenly he answered, 'He is not willing to believe harm of you.'

'Well then, and he is right,' Glenlyon cried, 'and you must

take counsel from him. After all, Alasdair, just ask yourself. Is it likely I would harm my own wife's kin – the people whose salt I have eaten these twelve days past? You do me injustice, lad, a great injustice.'

With a hand on Alasdair's shoulder he began moving to the door, manoeuvring the other with him and talking all the time, protesting his goodwill to the men of Glencoe and cursing the exigencies of Army life that hauled poor soldiers out in such weather to deal with a nuisance like Glengarry.

Alasdair went with him, still doubtful but unresisting, his angry suspicions smothering under the flow of innocent, friendly talk. He stepped out into the storm again. Glenlyon closed the door behind him, cutting off the blast of snow that had swept into the room with its opening. He leaned against the closed door, his back pressed against it, his tall form shaking in a paroxysm of silent laughter.

When he had recovered from this he stepped lightly to the table and lifted the wine-flask. He poured himself a cupful of wine and as he lifted it to his lips he looked sideways at me. Lips stretched in his thin, cat-like smile he said:

'A pity you will not drink with me, Ensign Stewart. There are still more than four hours to go before you put steel into Inverrigan.'

He drank and put the cup down. Still smiling he added, 'And it is going to be a cold night of waiting for you, Ensign – a long, cold night!'

8 Massacre

There was little movement and less conversation in the guard-room during the next few hours. The Corporal on duty at the door was relieved with each hourly changing of the guard. Lundie and Lindsay each made a further tour of inspection of the Inverrigan 2 and 3 guard-posts, but apart from this there was nothing for any of us to do except wait.

Lundie kept the fire supplied with peats and every so often he rose to trim the wick of the small stone lamp that hung from a bracket let into one of the walls. Lindsay continued to sit by the fire, leaning forward with his elbows on his knees and his clasped hands in front of him. There was no expression that I could see on Lundie's fleshy face, but Lindsay had a nervous twitching in one cheek which grew more pronounced with the passing of time until, by three o'clock, the whole of one side of his face was quivering in a manner most unpleasant to see.

Glenlyon ignored us all. He sat with his arms folded, his chin sunk on his chest and his gaze fixed on the watch lying on the table. Occasionally he lifted his head as if listening to the sound of the blizzard's raging, and frowned when he did so as though still disturbed by the effect it might have on his plans. The wine-flask by his elbow stood untouched after Alasdair's departure – a circumstance that both surprised and dismayed me since I had counted on his growing tipsy enough to fumble his actions when I made my break.

I still had no plan of escape in my mind and as the hours passed without an idea occurring to me I began to grow desperate. My hands trembled and there was a sickness in the pit of my stomach that rose into my throat and threatened to overwhelm me. I fought it down and clenched my hands to control their trembling. An opportunity would come, I told myself. An opportunity *must* come. Yet still nothing happened till the hands of Glenlyon's watch stood at half past three.

He stirred from his position then, and reaching inside his coat he drew out a silver flask of the kind used for carrying spirits. The smell of brandy reached me as he uncapped it, and using the top as a measure, served some out to the other two and then to himself. As if it had been the key all three of them had been waiting to unlock their speech, they began to talk after the first swallow of the brandy.

'You will leave at four o'clock,' Glenlyon said to Lindsay. 'Take a troop of six men with you. That will be enough to over-power him.'

'It will not be an easy task to kill him with cold steel,' Lundie said. 'MacIan is a big man, and strong for all his years.'

'Hold your tongue,' Lindsay told him roughly. 'He will die as quick as any other man would with half a dozen swords through him.'

He swallowed down the second measure of brandy Glenlyon handed him and glaring at Lundie he added, 'And remember, the old woman's jewels are mine!'

'Once *I* have had my pick of them,' Glenlyon reminded him. 'And make sure MacIan is properly dead before you snatch his lady's rings, or I will have the rank stripped from the pair of you!'

They went on talking, the brandy measure passing back and forth between them, their talk becoming looser, their references to the impending murder of MacIan become more brutal with the mounting effect of the spirits on their brains. I sat in silence, my mind reeling under the impact of the further horror their talk had revealed. And recalling the naked greed on Lindsay's face at his first sight of the beautiful rings worn by Lady Glencoe I was sickened more by the realization that, even as he was accepting the cup of wine from her hand, he had been planning murder to satisfy that greed.

I looked at the three of them, laughing and boasting as they drank the brandy and suddenly I realized why no wine had been drunk since Alasdair's departure and why they were drinking brandy now. A too-early indulgence in wine would have fuddled them for the event. The brandy so shortly before it was the stimulant they needed to heat their brains to the flash-point where conscience was consumed.

They were afraid of what they had to do! In spite of Glenlyon's desire for revenge, in spite of the greed of the other two, they were all still afraid of the moment when they would become murderers!

I left a boundless contempt for them in this realization, and following on it came a surge of hope. If these three who had something to gain from the massacre were thus nerving themselves to it, how much less willing would the common soldiery be to sin their souls with the deed! They might not dare to disobey orders openly, but might not some of them try to warn the victims beforehand?

There was hope also even in the dreadful mission with which Lundie and Lindsay had been entrusted, for once they had left the guard-post I would only have Glenlyon to deal with. That was the chance for which I had prayed and the silver flask of brandy had given me the idea I needed to take advantage of it. I kept my eyes cast down to hide the expression in them and under cover of the table I rapidly flexed the fingers and wrist of my right hand. A quick and supple gesture would be needed for what I planned to do.

'It is time,' Glenlyon said crisply. He gestured to the door and swung to keep his eyes fixed on me as the other two went out, crouching when the blast of the snow-laden wind caught them. I made no move to take advantage of the opening door. Glenlyon smiled to see me continuing to sit motionless and took his place opposite me again remarking, 'You are learning sense, young sir. May it long continue.'

He talked on and I let him talk, not listening to what he said but marking off time in my mind till I judged that the other two would have travelled far enough from the guard-post to allow me to break out of it unobserved by any save the Corporal on sentry-duty. When I thought this to be the case, I politely requested Glenlyon to allow me to rise and draw nearer the fire.

'I am cold with sitting so long in the one position, sir,' I explained.

Grinning he reminded me, 'I told you that it would be a long night.'

'Yes, sir,' I agreed. 'I would have been wise to take the wine you offered me.'

'Pride goes before a fall, eh?' Genially he teased me and pushed the wine-flask across the table. 'Have some now, Stewart Have some now.'

'If you would be so kind, sir,' I said humbly, 'a sup of brandy would be more the thing for this particular time.'

'Brandy?' he repeated. 'I never knew you to drink spirits before, Stewart.'

'No more I have, sir,' I agreed. 'But neither have I killed a man in cold blood before.'

He gave me a long, curious stare. 'You puzzle me, Stewart,' he said at length, and then caught himself up, 'No – I am wrong. You disappoint me! I would have sworn that you would have accepted a bullet in the heart rather than kill Inverrigan. So much for all your pretty talk about honour, eh?'

A moment longer he stared at me, his lip curling with amused contempt. I felt myself flushing with rage, but doubtless he took my colour for a flush of shame for he laughed as he poured a measure of brandy into the top of his flask and handed it to me. Our eyes met.

'To honour!' he said, raising the flask in a slight, mocking gesture towards me.

'To honour,' I repeated quietly, and with the quick turn of the wrist I had practised I dashed the contents of the flask-top into his eyes.

He screamed hoarsely as the strong spirit burned them. The flask dropped from his hands and he staggered back rubbing furiously at his face, but even as the scream left his lips I leapt for the door and pulled it sharply open. A wild whirl of snow enveloped me as I plunged through the opening, and blinded by it, I cannoned straight into the sentry outside.

Glenlyon's voice roaring, 'Stop him! Stop him!' reached us both at the moment of impact. Instantly I took up the cry, 'Stop him!' thrusting the bewildered sentry from me with a force that toppled him to the ground and rushing forward on my shout.

I ran blindly into the teeth of the storm for it was blowing from the east and Achnacon lay east of Inverrigan. I kept low as I ran for fear Glenlyon's rage would make him break his own ruling and shoot after me, but within a few seconds I knew that this danger had passed also. I could still hear his voice shouting behind me but the darkness and the driving snow combined to hide us from one another. Glenlyon had lost me.

Nor was there much danger of his trying to track me down for between the speed of my escape and his half-blinded condition at the time he could not have told the direction of my flight. The sentry could tell him nothing since he had been sprawling in the snow at the vital moment. The real danger for me now was that I might run into the patrol headed by Lundie and Lindsay on its way past Achnacon to MacIan's house in Glen Muidhe.

I had to risk this. My time was too short to allow of a detour away from the course they would be bound to take along the guiding line the River Coe made between Inverrigan and Achnacon. As for MacIan and his lady, I had no choice but to leave them to their fate. I could not hope to reach them before their murderers did if I stopped en route to rouse the people at Achnacon – as it was clearly my duty to do.

Struggling on as fast as I could in the face of the blizzard, I argued all this out with myself. Yet my heart was still heavy for MacIan and Lady Glencoe and I was fiercely glad that Glenlyon had ordered cold steel as the method of killing. Whatever the old Chief had ordered his men to do with their weapons, he had still kept his own mighty broadsword in plain view all the time we had spent in the glen, and outnumbered as he would be that night I was certain he would not fall without taking several of his murderers down with him. I hoped it would be Lundie and Lindsay who would die.

I saw their patrol ahead of me when I was only a few yards from it, so thick was the snow driving into my face. Immediately I swung away from the line of the river and plunged into a thicket of young birch trees some dozen yards from the river bank. With the force of the blizzard blowing in their faces the pace of the patrol was more of a plod than a march and I estimated that, if I could only force myself to keep up my own pace, I would be ahead of them by the time I had come to the end of the birch covert.

The trees broke the force of the wind for me but this advantage was cancelled out by the fact that the ground between them was uneven and boggy under its covering of snow. Yet still, my pace over all was faster than theirs for I had desperation to goad me to my best speed whereas Lindsay's men were moving at a rate that suited the time they had in hand to reach their objective.

I came out of the farther side of the birch thicket not knowing whether my reasoning on these lines had been correct, but assuming with relief that it must have been as I gained the river bank once more and after some minutes hard going had still not blundered into them again. I kept on at the same staggering run which had served me till then, the rushing sound of the river still my only guide through the wild drive of the snow in the darkness.

The wind tore with cold, cruel fingers at my face and scalp. It whipped my eyes with a million tiny scourges of driven snow and beat the breath from my body till I gasped and choked on the snow-laden stream of freezing air that rushed into my mouth. On the day of the hunt I thought I had been stretched to the last limit of my physical endurance, but as I fought the storm that night on the way to Achnacon I discovered agonies in my body I had never dreamed of.

Yet I could not give in to them. I could not lie down in the snow and die as my body screamed to be allowed to do, for my will was in command and every step I took was teaching me that the will recognizes no limits to the body's endurance. If I did pitch forward in my tracks and die of exhaustion – as I momentarily felt I would – this knowledge would be the last flicker of bitter glory my will would know before the body's weakness finally defeated it.

Achnacon rose before me as suddenly and unexpectedly as MacIan's death-patrol had done. Black hulks of houses stood solidly among the gusting snow, and among them the guardhouse with the lit windows which had revealed the hamlet to me. I pulled to a clumsy halt and stood with my labouring breath searing painfully in my chest while I tried to orient myself to the position of the house inhabited by Achnacon, the tacksman and leader of the little community.

It was bigger than the others. Round three sides of it ran a low dry-stone wall enclosing a cattle-fold, and I made for this so that I could approach the house from the rear and so remain unseen by any eyes watching from the guard-house. I knew from past experience that there was a door leading off the cattle-fold to the interior of the house and that I would be able to enter freely through it for, like all the other doors in the glen, it was never locked. Such was the measure of Highland hospitality, to friend or stranger alike.

I ran crouching along in the shelter of the wall, heaved myself over it in one quick scrambling movement, and dropped down into the sudden stillness of its shelter and the warmth rising from the packed bodies of the cattle huddling between it and the house. The cattle, small black bullocks for the beef-markets of the south, snorted and panicked from me then closed in to follow me curiously as I ran for the back door of the house. They stood in a snuffling semi-circle round me while I paused with my hand on the door-latch, hesitating before I committed myself to enter.

I was fairly sure there were no soldiers in Achnacon's house. At the time of the billeting, I remembered, his brother, John Macdonald had moved in to lodge with him and so had his fellow-tacksman, Achtriochtan. Three families in the one house would leave little available room for soldiers in addition, yet still I entered with the greatest possible caution. After all I had already endured I was determined not to be discovered in the very moment of warning for lack of this little extra care.

Like a shadow I passed through the hay-store and the dairy. In another outhouse there were obstacles such as barrels of beef in pickle and hanging sides of smoked salmon to put the silence of my passage in hazard. I managed to slip safely past them all and eased myself silently at last through the door that opened into the main room of the house.

It was faintly lit by the glow of a peat fire on the hearth. I made out the outline of a box bed in one corner with two night-capped female heads resting on the pillows, and on a pile of deerskins in front of the fire, two men lying wrapped in their plaids. If there were soldiers in the house they were not in this room.

I crept over to the men, knelt down and gently shook the nearer one. He came awake instantly, reared up as swift as an adder striking and gripped me by the throat with sinewy, choking hands. I let myself go limp, slumping over him. Our movements woke the other man. He sprang up, kicked the fire into life, and when he saw who was held captive drew his dirk with a muttered exclamation in Gaelic.

It was Achnacon who held me and his brother who had the dirk drawn on me. When Achnacon saw who it was and that I was both unarmed and safely covered by his brother's dirk, he let me go. I had come prepared with what I had to say and in a few brief sentences I had told them the position and delivered my warning.

'You know where the soldiers are billeted here and how many there are,' I finished. 'Rouse as many of your people as you can without letting the troops become aware of it. Let those who can, fight, and those who cannot, flee. It is your only hope, Achnacon.'

The women had wakened as I spoke and crept from the shelter of the box-bed. All four stood around me looking with bewildered eyes from one to the other when I stopped speaking. I had forgotten till then my own incredulity when I had first learned of the plan for the massacre, but I was bitterly reminded of it when Achnacon burst out:

'I do not believe it – Mr Stewart, I think you must be out of your wits!'

He fumbled inside his shirt and drew out a little deerskin pouch hung on a silver chain round his neck.

'See, I have here in this pouch an acknowledgment of the oath of allegiance I took away back in the summertime along with the other tacksmen of the clan. Glenlyon cannot go against this!'

I thrust my face into his and spoke with all the force at my command. 'That will not protect you or your people now, Achnacon. I tell you, I have seen the order for the massacre and I know it will be carried out!'

Still he looked at me disbelievingly and protested, 'But Glenlyon himself told Inverrigan that the oath we took would protect us against any Government action.'

There was no time to tell him all the ins and outs of the plot Glenlyon had explained to me. 'He lied!' I snapped and swung round to the women. 'Persuade him,' I commanded. 'If he will not save himself at least persuade him to give his tenants the chance of life. Save at least the women-folk and the children if you can!'

As one woman they turned from me and with a burst of rapid Gaelic speech passing between them they snatched shawls from hooks behind the door and hurried from the house. I made to follow them but John Macdonald caught me by the arm. Urgently he demanded:

'Do you swear this is true?'

'I risked my life and threw away my commission to warn you,' I told him bitterly.

His bewilderment was pathetic. 'To rise and murder us who are their hosts,' he muttered, ' 'Tis monstrous . . . a crime unheard of . . .' He searched my face with his eyes. '. . . yet that Barbour – he is a killer. *He* would do such a thing!'

'They *all* will,' I insisted. 'In the name of God, man, be warned!'

He nodded, suddenly convinced. 'No man of honour lightly takes God's name into his mouth and the Stewarts of Eilidh have always been honourable men. I will persuade my brother of his peril, and warn the people.'

I shook the hand he held out to me. 'And you?' he asked. 'Where do you go now?'

'To Carnoch, as quickly as I can,' I told him. 'They may already be roused there for Alasdair Og suspected something of this kind. Also, there is a Clan Donald man in our troop who would try to reach Alasdair in time – yet even if he has not I must go and do what I can.'

I had already wasted too much time. With a final backward glance at Achnacon still frowning his disbelief by the fire, I went rapidly out and retraced my way through the cattle-fold and over the wall. A quick glance round showed me glimmers of light coming from some of the windows that had previously been dark, and from the tail of my eye I saw shadowy figures slipping between the houses. The wives of Achnacon and his brother had been active in the few minutes since they left their own home, and I took to my heels again thanking God that women are by nature quicker-witted and more suspicious than men.

The wind was on my back as I travelled the return journey between Achnacon and Inverrigan. With the soft mass of new-fallen snow dragging at my footsteps I was blown along before it in a blundering run, and as quickly and completely as a dark dream vanishes on waking, Achnacon vanished into the night behind me.

I had no way of telling the exact time but I knew it could not be far off the five o'clock striking hour ordered by Major Duncanson. I knew also that I could not hope to reach Inverrigan, let alone Carnoch before this time, but if either MacEachern or Alasdair had roused the Carnoch people there might still be something I could do to help, and so I kept on running.

I was perhaps half a mile off Inverrigan when the darkness of the sky ahead of me flowered suddenly into fire. I saw houses silhouetted against the flames and realized that the fire had its source in Inverrigan. Immediately I broke away to my left, to the rising ground which makes the northern skirt of the mountain of Meall Mor. From there as I circled past the village I could see the confirmation of the fear the flames had bred in me. The massacre in Inverrigan was well under way.

There were at least six of the houses there ablaze, and even though I was some distance from them the flames were bright enough to show figures running through the village. The sound of screaming came faintly to me and mingled with this were sudden wild bursts of yelling. I could not bear to contemplate the meaning of these sounds. I clapped my hands over my ears to shut them out while I struggled against the impulse to run down to the village and try to use my authority as an officer in an attempt to stop some of the killing.

With Glenlyon in command, however, I knew it could only be a matter of minutes before I was found at this device and pistolled for my pains. My life could still be more worth to the Macdonalds than a heroic gesture and so, cursing Glenlyon with a savagery I had not known I could feel, I completed my circle of Inverrigan and ran on to Carnoch.

I was still less than halfway there when the red-coat soldier came looming at me through the still thickly-falling snow. There was no time to feel fear. For a flashing second only I glimpsed the raised musket in his hands before it came smashing butt first across my shoulder and the side of my head. I was spun violently sideways by the blow and as I fell to the snow the feeling uppermost in my mind was one of annoyance at my own stupidity.

I should have counted on Glenlyon setting such a trap for me!

I was dazed by the blow but the thick, upturned collar of my coat had saved me from its full force. My training also came to the aid of my dizzied mind and I rolled sidewards from the path of the bayonet-thrust that came stabbing down at me. As I rolled I had a swift impression of the build of the fellow who had attacked me, and banking everything on the sudden wild hope this glimpse inspired, I yelled:

'MacEachern! It is Stewart – Ensign Stewart! Hold your hand, MacEachern!'

The poised figure above me froze with bayonet drawn back for a second thrust, then abruptly its tense outline slackened and the man flopped down beside me in the snow. He brought his face close to mine to peer at me, and with hot breath fanning my cheek he whispered:

'Dear God, it is Mr Stewart!'

Quickly he slid an arm round my shoulders and in great distress as he helped me to rise he exclaimed, 'God forgive me, sir, I would have killed you for sure if you had not called out who you were!'

Clinging to him to steady myself I asked, 'Why did you attack me, MacEachern?'

'I thought I had stumbled into a patrol sent out to re-capture me, sir,' he explained.

I laughed weakly. 'And I thought the same! I am on the run too, MacEachern.'

'Eh?' In his astonishment he released his grip on me. I groped for the support of a boulder beside the track, and then realizing it was one of a great tumble of rocks I told him.

'Get down behind these rocks with me or the same danger may overtake us both again while we stand talking.'

I scrambled into cover and he came to crouch down beside me. 'I was put into custody you see, sir—' he began but I interrupted him, 'I know that and I can see that you have escaped. Tell me first if you know what has been happening at Carnoch.'

'Major Duncanson's men are there now,' he told me, 'but I think they will be marching towards Inverrigan soon for they have been disappointed of much of their prey at Carnoch.'

'Ah! So you managed to warn them?'

'No, sir, it was Alasdair and Mistress Elspeth who roused the people there. They were both awake and on watch when I ran to his house like you told me to do. They ran to warn the village while I went at Alasdair's bidding to the house of his brother John. I roused a servant there and shouted to him to pass the warning to his master. I saw Duncanson's men approaching Alasdair's house even while I spoke with the servant. And so I lingered, knowing they would come straight to John's house when they found Alasdair missing and hoping to lead them on a false trail. They were not twenty yards from it when he broke free by a back door and escaped up the side of Meall Mor with his wife and a nurse-woman holding their child. I set up a great shout then, pretending to be one of Sergeant Hendrie's men sent to lead them to a cattle-fold where I swore John had been seen taking refuge.'

'And then?'

'Oh, then sir, I lost them in the darkness and confusion of cattle there, as I had meant to do. After that I ran back towards Carnoch and met Alasdair on the way with a gathering of people he had saved from Sergeant Hendrie's men. I told him of the false trail I had laid for Duncanson's troop and warned him that both ends of the glen were netted, and at that he began urging his people to make up the side of Meall Mor as fast as they could and then to gather in Glen Muidhe.'

'How many casualties?' I asked. 'Did you ask Alasdair?'

'Yes, sir, but he said it had all been too dark and confused to tell. And he was greatly put about too because Mistress Elspeth had been wounded by a sword-thrust.'

I sat for a few moments thinking what he had said, and then with a sigh I told him, 'You have done well – very well,

MacEachern. Tell me now how you managed to escape in the first place.'

'Oh, that was no trouble, sir,' he explained. 'The place they put me in had earthen walls and all I did was to pick away at one till I had a hole big enough to crawl through. Then I crept up behind a sentry, knocked him over the head, and stole his pistol and musket.'

I was amused, in spite of our situation, at the calm way he said this, and grinning at him in the darkness I asked, 'But why were you running back to Inverrigan then, when we met so abruptly?'

'I – I hoped to find you, sir,' he said awkwardly. 'I am for court-martial if they capture me and I thought – I thought you might speak up for me. About that order you gave me, you understand and – and a gentleman like you, if you were to speak up for me – if you would, sir—'

I felt the grin fading off my face as his voice stammered on. Indeed, for a moment I could almost have wept for the poor, brave, silly creature!

'Wait, wait, MacEachern,' I interrupted him. 'You have not heard my story.'

I gave him a brief account of my own rebellion, and then as gently as I could, I explained how I had come to give him the order to warn Alasdair.

'But it would have made no difference even if I had believed in your vision,' I added, 'for, as matters have turned out, you can see that I had no more right to give you that order than you had to carry the warning. We are both equally for court-martial now, my poor fellow.'

He made no answer to this and then, after several moments of silence he asked humbly, 'What must I do then, sir?'

I stood up. 'On your feet, MacEachern,' I ordered briskly. 'We will make for Glen Muidhe.'

'Glen Muidhe, sir?'

'Why do you think Alasdair was urging his people to gather there?' I asked. 'The route to Glen Creran lies by Glen Muidhe, and the Stewarts of Glen Creran are friendly to the Glencoe Macdonalds. Furthermore, an escape by the steep climb through the Lairig Gartain or the Lairig Eilde would only be possible in this weather for strong young huntsmen, and there are women and children to be saved.'

MacEachern scrambled to his feet. 'And you think *we* can escape through Glen Muidhe with the Macdonalds, sir?'

'If it is possible, we will,' I told him. 'But do not count on it, MacEachern, for we have still a duty towards the survivors of the massacre. We must help to cover their escape if we can before we think of our own.'

I held out my hand to him. 'Will you lend me your pistol? Unlike you, I did not manage to secure a weapon when I escaped.'

'Gladly, sir!' He drew his pistol and handed it to me. I turned it over in my hand as he was fumbling in his ammunition pouch to find ball and powder for it, and confidence flowed into me from the smooth feel of the butt against my palm.

The pistol was a Government issue one and therefore a far cry from the fine weapon I had inherited from my father. It was still a well-made firing-piece, however, and with it in my hand I felt some of my soldierly pride returning to me. After all, I thought, I was still an officer. I still had the habit of command. And now that I had a weapon I was no longer completely at the mercy of every chance element in my situation.

9 Death patrol

'We had better keep well up above the level of the track,' I told MacEachern, and led the way up the side of Meall Mor.

It was difficult work climbing the snow-covered slope and then scrambling along on the traverse towards Glen Muidhe, but it was the only sure way of avoiding troops patrolling through the glen and so we persevered at the level I had chosen.

At intervals through the veils of snow swirling across the mountain-face we thought we could make out an occasional dark shape labouring in the same eastwards direction. We heard voices calling, thin and desolate through the howling of the wind, and once we heard a baby's cry that was cut off abruptly as if someone had clapped a hand over the child's face.

It occurred to me that our uniforms might put us in immediate danger of death if we ran into any armed men among these survivors of the massacre, for they would have no way of telling at first that we were not in pursuit of them. I warned MacEachern accordingly, and told him to be ready to cry out in Gaelic some notice of our friendly intentions.

Ahead of us in the valley the blaze from Inverrigan leapt ever higher and wider against the surrounding dark. Achnacon was on fire too. We saw the glow from its flames on the horizon of our vision as we passed above Inverrigan and the full blaze of it came into our view when we rounded the shoulder of Meall Mor and began to traverse that part of it which overlooks Glen Muidhe.

Near at hand our vision was still limited by the blizzard. We could see no sign of any gathering of survivors and so I led the way downwards in search of them. Within a few minutes voices came faintly to us again, and following the sound of these we began to discern small groups of people huddled in the snow. The farther down we went the bigger and more numerous grew these groups, and gradually the full plight of the surviving Macdonalds began to open out to us.

The men, women and children who were scattered in all directions over the eastern slope of Meall Mor were exposed to the full blast of the blizzard. They crouched in their little groups with the men bracing themselves as wind-breaks for the women, and the women trying to shelter the children under their shawls. Many of the people were bare-foot and half-naked as they had leapt from their beds, and from the children there came a countinuous low moaning and whimpering that was most distressing to hear.

They would die there in the snow, I thought, unless they were got quickly on the move! And throwing all caution aside I roared at the top of my voice,

'*Alasdair Og MacIan! Answer me, Alasdair! Where are you?*'

'Here! Here!' a voice called. 'Over here, beside John!'

As fast as I could I stumbled towards the voice, and found myself in the midst of a group of some twenty people. I pressed through them calling out, 'I had no part in the murder, Alasdair. I am on the run from Glenlyon.'

MacEachern also called out in Gaelic the friendly assurances I had told him to give, and though there were mutters of anger and alarm as the people became aware of the shape of our uniforms they still fell back to let us through. I saw Alasdair kneeling at the centre of the group with John standing beside him. Mistress Elspeth lay at John's feet on a bundle of plaids, a blood-stained bandage round her chest. I peered over Alasdair's shoulder as he rose to meet me and softly inquired,

'Is she alive?'

'For the moment,' he answered, his face still startled to see it was really myself there. 'She has had a sword-thrust through her.'

'How do *you* come to be here? What do you want?' John followed up Alasdair's words sharply.

'I am on the run. I refused Glenlyon's order for the massacre. I tried to warn as many of your people as possible of it.'

The explanation came tumbling hurriedly out of me at the expression of menace on John's face, and as hurriedly, MacEachern added,

'It was Mr Stewart told me to warn your brother, sir. You would not have got away but for him.'

'Stewart must be speaking the truth, John. This man with him is the fellow who brought me the warning,' Alasdair said, and I gave John no time to dispute this.

'You must get the people on the move to Glen Creran or they will die here,' I said urgently. 'MacEachern and I are armed. If you wish, we will try to delay any troops that pursue you.'

'We were just about to move,' Alasdair told me. 'John has been herding in the stragglers while I bandaged Elspeth.'

Impulsively he held out his hand. 'I thank God you had no part in this, Robert!'

'I did not know—' I began, and was rudely interrupted by shouts and commotion in the crowd around us. It swayed and parted and a man came staggering through. His face was streaked with blood and blood soaked the front of his shirt. He fell on his knees beside us grasping at Alasdair's plaid as he did so, and through the mask of blood that covered them I recognized the features of John Macdonald, Achnacon's brother.

To the questions that showered down on him I added my own demand to know what had happened after I left him in Achnacon's house. He raised his face to mine, recognized me, and gasped out,

'Achnacon is dead – shot—'

'Shot!' I exclaimed. 'But Glenlyon's orders were to use cold steel—'

The wounded man gasped on, not heeding my interruption '—six others shot with him. He – would not believe – gathered the men to talk with him in his house. I locked the doors. Barbour – surrounded the house and fired a volley through the windows. All killed, except me—'

'We have many of the women and children from Achnacon safe here,' John told him gently. 'How was it they escaped?'

The wounded man gestured feebly to me. 'He – brought warning. My wife and – Achnacon's wife carried it to the people.'

'And how do you come to be the only one left alive from Barbour's volley?' I asked wonderingly.

'I was wounded. Barbour found me alive when he broke into the house.' He swayed, and both Alasdair and I caught him and lowered him carefully to the ground. He looked up at us and whispered, 'I begged him for the favour of dying under the open sky. He laughed. He said, *"I will pay you for my fortnight's meat with that favour."* '

I looked across him to Alasdair and knew that the look of horror on his face matched my own. The Macdonald went on whispering.

'He stood me in front of a firing-squad. I leapt forward – threw my plaid over the muzzles of their rifles – then – I ran. I lost much blood but I kept on running – running . . .'

His voice tailed away. Alasdair looked up and called for something to bind his wounds and I rose to my feet thinking savagely. *'So Barbour could not resist the excuse the locked doors gave him for using his precious muskets!'* A woman came forward with a length of cloth in her hand. I left Alasdair to bind the man's wounds and followed John as he moved out of the group and beckoned me with him. Catching my arm he asked quietly:

'What has happened to my father and mother? Can you tell me?'

There was no time to spare for breaking the news gently. I told him what I knew and his face grew even bleaker than it had been before.

All he said, however, was, 'We will soon know if Lindsay's troop succeeded in killing MacIan. I have sent some of the young men on to his house to find out what they could. Now we must get started. We must reach the water-shed into Glen Creran before daylight discovers us to the red-coats.'

I moved among the people with him, listening to his commands and helping where I could to reduce the chaos of weeping women and bewildered men into some sort of marching order. A boy of some thirteen years broke out of one group and threw himself at John's feet, sobbing and imploring him in Gaelic for some favour. I recognized him as the elder of the two boys in the household where I had found MacEachern telling the tale of the giant, and looked round for him to interpret the boy's babbling.

He had followed John and myself and was at my shoulder, listening wide-eyed to the flood of Gaelic speech. As John bent to pull the boy to his feet I asked him what had been said and he exclaimed,

' 'Tis his little brother Seumas, sir – you remember him? – the boy with the Book of Tales. This boy says he escaped with Seumas when Glenlyon's men came, but the little fellow cried and said he must go back for his Book of Tales and ran from him, back to Inverrigan. Both their parents were killed by Glenlyon's men, and the boy is pleading the Chief's son to help him find someone who will go back to Inverrigan with him to look for his little brother.'

I stared at MacEachern, remembering with pain the small, eager figure thrusting the precious Book of Tales at me, and abruptly I made a decision. 'I am going back to look for the boy,' I told him.

His face, that had been drawn with the same pain of remembering, lit up in a wide grin. His hand came up in salute and he said happily,

'Beg permission to go with you, sir!'

I was only too glad to have him with me and told him so, and still grinning as if I had offered him a bounty instead of a dangerous mission he saluted again with a smart, 'Sir!'

'John—!' I caught the attention of MacIan's son. 'Tell the boy that MacEachern and I are going back to look for his brother. And besides—' the thought occurred to me as I spoke, '—we will make it an opportunity to try and discover whether they mean to send out patrols to try and track down the survivors.'

John made no argument. 'The honour is all the greater in that you take our danger on you as well as your own,' he said gravely.

I left him speaking to the boy and with MacEachern at my side started back for Inverrigan.

'We will take a line on the boy's house from the road and go down to it together,' I instructed him. 'If he is not hiding in some cover there we will separate and you will search the village to the east while I search it to the west.'

'You will have the longer distance to travel back to Glen

117

Muidhe if you take the west side, sir,' he objected, 'and so you will run the greater risk of discovery.'

'That is only right,' I told him sharply. 'As an officer it is my duty to take the more dangerous part of the enterprise.'

We scrambled along together in silence for several minutes and then, suddenly and quietly, he said, 'You are a brave laddie but you are a stubborn one too – sir!'

I was so astonished at the idea of a private soldier daring to make such a comment to an officer that I could think of nothing to say at first, and by the time I had thought of a reprimand it seemed heartless to deliver it to one who had freely elected to face danger with me. I let his presumption pass, therefore, and went on with my instructions.

'Do not run if you come under the observation of any Government troops after we separate,' I told him. 'You will be wiser to pretend boldly that you are engaged on the same work as they are. We will take the first opportunity we can to disguise our features by blackening them with some suitable material, and you must also hide as much of your face as possible with your hat pulled down and your coat-collar turned up.'

'Yes, sir,' he said obediently, and then after a pause, 'You can rely on me, sir.'

Indeed I could, I thought to myself with not a little surprise in the realization. Private MacEachern was certainly only a rough, ignorant fellow but he was also showing himself to be much less of a fool than I had supposed!

We reached the point where I had decided we must go down to the village and I gave him my last instruction.

'Do not wait for me once you have scoured your part of the village,' I ordered. 'Make your own way as speedily as you can back to Glen Muidhe, and re-join the Macdonalds. And find yourself a plaid or some such thing to wear as a disguise over your uniform before you do so. The escape party may have scouts bringing up their rear who will otherwise take you for part of a pursuing patrol.'

'I will find a disguise, sir,' he answered, 'but I will not go back to Glen Muidhe without you.'

'You stubborn fool! I gave you an order. Obey it, or I will—'

I stopped short, feeling foolish. There was nothing I could do to MacEachern if he chose to disobey me.

'You spoke of what was due from your rank, sir,' he said reproachfully. 'What of *my* duty? Am I not bound to stand by my officer?'

From this attitude I could not shift him and at last I gave up the argument and saved my breath for the scramble down to the road running past Inverrigan. It had recently been travelled by a considerable body of men, I noted. Their feet had beaten a broad track through the soft new snow, and this track swung away from the main one and down to Inverrigan. Some at least of Duncanson's men had arrived there from Carnoch.

The boy's house was near No. 1 guard-post. We lined ourselves up on this and advanced cautiously towards the houses. At least half of them were in flames and the whole scattered area of the village was a wild pattern of red, leaping light chequered with irregular patches of black shadow. There were figures running backwards and forwards between the houses – the figures of red-coat soldiers. The crackling and roaring of the flames and the yells of the red-coats as they appeared suddenly from the shadows and leaped forward into the light made them seem like demons rejoicing in some inferno. I prickled with goose-flesh at the sight and at the thought of the small boy trapped somewhere at the heart of it.

'*Put all to the sword under seventy,*' the order had said. The boy's tender years would not save him from the bayonets of the soldiers searching the houses that had not yet been fired!

There was charred wood in plenty lying around. Rapidly we blacked our faces with some of this, then keeping close together and slipping warily from one patch of shadow to the next, we began our search. Each time we came to an undamaged house MacEachern went in and called the boy's name, softly coaxing him in Gaelic to come forth if he was hiding there. I stood guard while he did this then we moved on again, our eyes probing the shadows cast by peat-stack and out-houses, all our senses alert for a sudden irruption of troops into our immediate vicinity.

Beside a house where the flames had not yet got a strong hold MacEachern pulled me up sharply, his breath hissing between his teeth. His grip like iron on my shoulder, he pointed to the trampled snow in front of the threshold. In the pale glow of flame from the open door I saw a great red smear of blood on the dirty white of the snow, and lying at the edge of the smear, a baby's hand severed at the wrist.

MacEachern was trembling so violently that I thought he must be going into a convulsion.

'I saw it – I saw it in my vision,' he whispered thickly, 'and now I see it plain! God help me – I see it plain!'

'Bear up, man, bear up!' I shook him fiercely. 'I will search this house. You keep watch.'

I crossed the threshold of the house, fighting down a choking sickness in my throat as I stepped over the tiny, curled fingers of the hand. Steeling myself to whatever I might find I cast quickly round as much as I could of the burning interior. There was no one there, and no bodies that I could see. I gave silent thanks for having been spared the sight of the one I had dreaded to find, and returned to MacEachern.

'Listen, sir!' he whispered as I came out.

There was now only a group of three houses between us and the guard-post and from beyond these we could hear a voice raised in a fury of invective above the shouts of the mopping-up parties and the sound of the burning houses.

'Duncanson!' I whispered. ' 'Tis Duncanson's voice!'

This could be an opportunity to find out what plans were toward, I thought. I whispered the thought to MacEachern and motioned him forward with me. We crossed a lit space at a run and gained the shelter of the shadow cast by the nearest of the group of three houses. Creeping round its walls we ran crouching across the space between it and the other two, and plunged down behind the cover of a peat-stack piled up against the wall of the furthest one.

Peering cautiously over this I found myself looking out over an open space with the guard-post to my right and Inverrigan's house directly ahead of me. Flames were leaping from it and from another house to its left, and these flames lit the space and the figures in it like actors on a stage.

A crowd of nearly fifty soldiers stood leaning on their muskets on the far right of the space. In the centre of it, piled up in a heap, lay the corpses of a number of men. I counted nine of them. Their hands were bound, and the man hanging head downward from the top of the pile was Inverrigan himself.

Like the three principal actors in this ghastly drama, Major Duncanson, Captain Drummond and Captain Robert Campbell of Glenlyon stood beside the pile of corpses. Major Duncanson was shaking his fist under Glenlyon's nose and reviling him at the top of his voice for having bungled his orders.

'They were to be wiped out – the whole clan was to be destroyed;' he screamed as I poked my head from cover. 'And what do I find here at Inverrigan? Nine corpses! Nine only! You will pay for this you miserable drunken fool! You will not be *Captain* Campbell for long when I report of this to higher authority!'

Glenlyon had stood during this ranting with his hands hanging loosely at his sides, his pistol drooping from the slack fingers of his right hand, his chin sunk on his chest. Now he looked up, and I was near enough him to see that his face was as haggard as that of a man waking from a nightmare.

'Let be, sir, let be,' he said hoarsely. 'I am human. I needed the brandy to fire me to the deed.'

'It did not fire you enough,' Duncanson shouted, and would have said more but for a commotion out of the range of my vision. He swung towards its direction, as did everyone else there. I heard a further burst of the yelling that had broken into his speech, and from beyond Inverrigan's house a party of soldiers came running forward dragging a young Macdonald clansman with them.

They ran up to the group of officers and forced the young man to his knees in front of them. He was naked except for a plaid girded loosely round his waist, and his bare chest was streaked with blood from a wound in his shoulder. A soldier gripped his hair, pulling his head back to stare up at Glenlyon, and with a thrill of horror that tingled every nerve I recognized the face of the young huntsman I had saved from the hooves of the stag in Glen Muidhe. Duncanson planted his arms akimbo and stared from the young man to Glenlyon.

'Prove yourself, Glenlyon,' he said harshly. 'Prove you have not failed in your duty to the Crown by pistolling this fellow. Now!'

Glenlyon's slack grip tightened convulsively on his pistol. I drew in a gasping breath, my own hands clenching involuntarily at his gesture. Now I knew that this young man who had called me by that name was indeed my brother, and with all the force of my mind I willed Glenlyon not to shoot.

His pistol hand came slowly up to waist-level. The Macdonald knelt staring up at him without a word or movement, Glenlyon's aim wavered.

'No!' he cried sharply. His hand dropped down and the pistol swung loosely from it again. He turned away, his other hand raised to hide his face. 'I have had enough of killing! I am sickened of corpses!'

My eyes were on Glenlyon and it was only from the tail of my vision that I saw Duncanson's hand swing up. The pistol in it cracked sharply. The young huntsman jerked backwards, hung rigid for a second with the bullet-hole in his forehead showing like a round black O, and then fell face down at Duncanson's feet.

A silence followed, a silence that seemed to blanket even the roar of the flames. The shifting scene of the officers and soldiers in the open space seemed to freeze into a tableau in the curious distortion of time imposed by that fragment of silence. I became aware of MacEachern breathing heavily behind me in it, and then the silence was broken by a long, shrill scream of terror.

The small, darting figure of a child appeared seemingly from nowhere and, like a trapped animal, dashed wildly back and forth within the open space. He was pursued by two soldiers, swearing and laughing as he squirmed and dodged away from their grasp, and all the time as he sought frantically for escape he was clutching a book to his chest. It was Seumas, the boy we had come to find.

MacEachern's iron grip descended on my shoulder again and I whispered a quick reply to the question it asked.

'No! We would throw away our lives uselessly. We cannot save him now.'

One of the boy's turns brought him close to the group of officers. He hesitated for a fraction of time and then, recognizing Glenlyon's face, threw himself at his feet and clutched him round the knees. Screaming and crying he clung there, his face imploringly upturned, his precious Book of Tales still clutched in the same grip that held Glenlyon's knees. The pursuing soldiers stopped short, hesitating to drag him from an officer. Duncanson stroked his chin, waiting to see what Glenlyon would do. Drummond roared,

'Pistol him, Glenlyon!'

Glenlyon swayed above the boy, his face dazed and blank. I felt MacEachern rise to his feet behind me and clutched at his coat to pull him down. Drummond's hand flashed up and the dirk in it flickered redly in the firelight as he brought it plunging down into the child's neck.

As Drummond's hand swung, MacEachern broke free from me with a roar and a leap that carried him running towards the scene. Drummond's head, bent forward to follow the downward thrust of his arm, would have taken the impact of his clubbed musket if Glenlyon in the same instant had not brought his pistol flashing up to fire. MacEachern was caught at the full stretch of his upward swing with the musket. He whirled, his musket falling from his hands, and his body dropped like a stone beside the body of the dead boy sagging from Glenlyon's knees.

The moment dissolved in confusion, with Duncanson shouting to know the meaning of MacEachern's action and Glenlyon cutting across his volley of questions with the explanation that the man was a rebel and a deserter. He was as eager now as he had been dull before and it was clear that he felt the saving of Drummond's life would go far to vindicate his poor showing in the massacre.

'There was another rebel, sir – an officer—' he added excitedly.

'An *officer*?' Duncanson interrupted, his face incredulous.

'Yes, sir. Ensign Stewart. He may have joined forces with this man, and if so—'

I did not wait to hear any more. Rapidly backing from my hiding-place, I made off eastwards through the village, and even as I did so I heard shouted orders for a search being issued to the soldiers. As I had done earlier I kept to shadow where I could and carefully reconnoitred every lit space before I crossed it, yet for all my care I was still not quick enough to avoid being seen by a patrol of some twenty soldiers which appeared suddenly from behind one of the houses.

Our surprise was mutual but I managed to keep my wits about me and began instantly to run towards them, shouting and waving my arms. The soldiers halted at this sudden sight of an officer running in such apparent excitement. I kept up my shouting till I had drawn level with the patrol then, without breaking my stride, I rushed past it half-turning as I did so to point back the way I had come.

'Over there, quickly, you men!' I shouted. 'A party of armed rebels is engaging!'

They broke into a run, the Corporal in charge urging them on, and I hoped their juncture with Duncanson's men would create confusion among the search-parties that were being mustered. I had underestimated Major Duncanson, however.

My course through the village was necessarily an irregular one because of the way I had been forced to take cover where I could. He must have guessed that this would be the case and instantly detailed patrols to surround the area of the village, but it was only when I was preparing to break free of the last of the houses that I discovered this stratagem.

I heard splashing sounds that warned me of men crossing the line of great boulders which made stepping-stones across the point where the River Coe made a loop to form the eastern boundary of the village. Following this came the voice of the Corporal in charge calling to his men to stand fast and be ready for me to break out of cover, and I knew I was trapped. I stood in the shadow debating my position.

The blizzard had slackened its force somewhat by this time, and although the snow was still driving down it was not the impenetrable curtain it had been earlier. Moreover, the soldiers waiting for me had their backs to the wind and would therefore have a longer range of vision through the snow than I would have with it driving into my face.

I could not hope to make an open break through their cordon without being seen by at least one of them, and when that happened they would combine to hunt me down relentlessly. That meant the escape route of Glen Muidhe would be closed to me for I could not risk drawing the hunt for me on to the trail of the Macdonalds' escape-party. There was an alternative course open to me, however, and the mere thought of what it involved so appalled even myself that I was sure Duncanson's men would never guess me to be capable of such foolhardiness.

The river! I whispered the words over to myself, shuddering already at the thought of the Coe's icy waters closing over me. It was only a few yards from me at this point. The rushing sound of it was loud in my ears. If I could slip quietly from pool to pool between its high rocky banks, I would be able to escape unseen through the cordon.

I knew I could not afford to hesitate on the decision or my nerve would fail me. Quickly I whipped off my cravat and tied my pistol and powder-bag up in it, then dropping to the ground I wormed my way towards the river-bank. I had no knowledge of the depth of the water at the point where I lowered myself in. All I could do was to hang on to the bank with one hand and keep the other with the pistol and powder-bag pouched in my cravat raised above the level of the water that received me.

I sank waist-deep before my feet touched bottom. I bit off the gasp of shock the chill of the water forced from me, lowered myself till there was only my head and pistol hand clear of the water and began to work my way upstream.

The level of the Coe onwards from my point of entry varied between a fast-flowing run of about a foot deep over straight stretches of a few yards long, and pools where the depth could have been six feet or more since my feet could not touch bottom there. I had to crawl and swim alternately, therefore, and of necessity moved so slowly that I had full opportunity to feel the cold of the water biting into my bones.

The stepping-stones would be my token that success was in my grasp. I would not have to travel far beyond them to be sure I had passed through the cordon. It could not have taken me much more than ten minutes to reach them, even at my slow pace, but it seemed a lifetime of misery to me. I slid through between two of the great flat-topped boulders, gritting my teeth to endure the last of the ordeal.

One of the straight, shallow runnels lay beyond the stepping-stones. I crawled along this and into a foam of rapids where I had to flop and slither on my belly over a jumble of small, rounded boulders. The rapids flowed out of a deep pool. I paused before plunging into it, to recover my breath and to ease the ache in my right wrist caused by the effort to keep my improvised pistol-pouch raised above the water.

At last I was ready to cross the pool, I did so, swimming one-handed, and bore into the bank on the far side of it. Even if I was not free of the cordon now I knew I could endure this strain no further, and I began the long painful business of hauling myself out on to the bank again.

I lay there panting and sick with the effort I had put out, and if Duncanson himself had come on me then I could not have moved for a king's ransom. Gradually the breath began to come back into my bruised body and as my breathing eased the thundering of my own heart ceased to deafen me. I raised my head and listened and at last I heard the faint sound of voices. They came from behind me.

I sat up, untied the pistol and powder-bag from my cravat and examined them. They were dry, and I had passed through the cordon. Now I could make for Glen Muidhe.

10 Survival trail

I had been given no opportunity to acquire a plaid to disguise my uniform as I had warned poor MacEachern he must do, but the tide of luck which had carried me so far still had some way to run in my favour that night.

I had not gone far up Glen Muidhe when I came on a plaid which some fleeing Macdonald must have dropped in the snow. I seized on it gladly and shook the powdery crust of snow-flakes from it. Then I stripped off my sodden clothes – a task which was by no means easy since my fingers were so stiff with cold as to be almost useless.

I kilted the plaid round my middle in the manner of High-land men, and disposed of the rest of its considerable length over as much of my upper body as possible. My arms and legs were still left bare by this arrangement and I was delighted to find that this did not detract from the general warmth impar-ted by the soft woollen folds of the plaid. The hunt had taught me how practical this dress was for active men in moun-tainous country. Now, I thought, I was learning also how well suited it was to combat the worst rigours of mountain weather.

My uniform coat was something I dared not leave lying openly behind me for its brilliant red against the snow when daylight came would give any searching patrol an obvious guide to the line of my flight. I buried it deep in snow, there-fore, resolutely stifling the sharp pangs of regret for the hopes and ambitions I was burying with it. There was no room in my situation for such self-indulgence, I told myself. I had to face up completely to the reality of being a rebel, a deserter and a fugitive from that night forward.

In this frame of mind I headed on up the glen, pondering how much distance the fleeing Macdonalds had managed to put between themselves and Glencoe. They were certain to be moving slowly for their numbers were made up of all sorts and conditions of people, from babes-in-arms to old men. Furthermore, the only way they could avoid the danger of pursuing patrols would be to travel at a fairly high level along the side of Meall Mor.

Their ultimate safety, of course – in so far as they could ever hope to be safe again – lay in reaching the water-shed between Glencoe and Glen Creran before daylight broke and revealed them still climbing towards this point. It would take very strong leadership on John's part to achieve this, I thought. Alasdair's fiery nature might have made him the fitter man to command such a situation, but Alasdair had a seriously-wounded wife to care for, and in any case, the people would not have accepted him for their leader. John was their Chief, now that MacIan was dead.

But *was* MacIan dead? I remembered the two cowardly men fortified by brandy who had set out to kill him, and I wondered. Could they possibly have succeeded in killing that massive old warrior with cold steel as Glenlyon had ordered? Was there even a hope that it was he who was leading his clansmen to safety while Lundie and Lindsay lay dead in the farm-house in Glen Muidhe?

The idea so excited me that I stopped and stared down into the valley dropping away to my left. MacIan's house lay almost directly below me, I estimated. It would not delay me long in catching up with the Macdonalds if I went down there to investigate.

It was a foolish impulse, rooted basely in curiosity and hatred of the two men who had been my fellow-officers, but nevertheless I obeyed it and began rapidly working my way down the mountainside. The closer I came to the floor of the glen the more convinced I was that I could see a light of some kind gleaming there, and hope rose in me at the prospect of finding this to be so. Light seemed to me to imply life, and there was no other house than MacIan's there.

I reached the house at last and stood looking at the faint gleam that came from one window of it. The door to the house stood open but there was no sign of life of any kind about the place, and now I was not so sure that I had read the meaning of the light correctly. Cautiously, I approached. My footsteps were silent in the snow but I still kept my pistol cocked, ready for use. If there were red-coats there I could be walking into a trap.

The room in which MacIan and his lady slept lay to the right of the open front door and it was from this room that the light came. I edged my way into it, pistol at the ready. The light came from a candle placed on a table by the bed in one corner of the room. It lit the place but poorly and at first I could not distinguish the identity of the man who lay sprawled face down on the floor. I lifted the candle and bent towards the body. It was MacIan, and he had not been killed by the sword. He had been shot twice – in the back.

I straightened up and held the candle high to examine the room. There was no one else there. The covers were thrown back on either side of the bed as they must have been when MacIan and his lady had risen from it. The Chief himself was dressed in shirt and trews, and wondering what could be deduced from these facts I set out to examine the rest of the house.

In the pantry I found the body of a serving-man sprawled on the floor. An ale-jug, the contents spilled from it, lay by his right hand, and on his left side were scattered a tray and three of Lady Glencoe's silver cups. I stood staring down at them as I pieced the fragments of the puzzle together.

MacIan had been roused from his bed by the arrival of Lundie and Lindsay, and he had evidently called the servant to bring ale for them while he dressed. They must have spoken him fair for him to have given this order – so fair that he had felt no fear of turning his back on them. And then they had shot him.

Even backed by their troop of six men they had not dared to face MacIan's sword. And not even with pistols in their hands had they dared to kill him face to face!

'Cowards!' I whispered savagely. 'Low, mean, murdering cowards!'

And where was Lady Glencoe? I lifted the candle and began another search of the house, calling her name softly as I went. No one answered me and I went outside eventually to search the out-houses. I found no trace of Lady Glencoe there either, but on a heap of refuse beside one of the out-houses I came upon the bodies of two more servants. They, also, had been shot. The snow that lay white and unmelting on their upturned faces showed that they had been dead for some time, and even if Lady Glencoe had escaped unwounded from the house she could not have been clad to survive for long in the raging white wilderness of the blizzard.

Sadly thinking of her many kindnesses to me, I turned away towards Meall Mor again.

I put out my best speed to make up for the time I had lost and some distance down the little glen that links Glen Muidhe to Glen Creran I caught up with the survivors' party. Alasdair was at the rear of it, encouraging the stragglers on and helping the weaker ones who had fallen behind to catch up with the main body again. I spoke briefly to him, asking for Mistress Elspeth. She was being carried by two young men farther forward in the line, he told me, and from his tone I realized that he did not expect her to survive the journey.

I moved forward to find John. All round me were people floundering desperately through the clinging snow, some falling and too feeble to rise again, men with small children perched on their shoulders pulling and tugging women and elderly people through the drifts and over the jutting rocks. Cries for help came echoing through the darkness, and once there was a despairing scream as a woman lost her footing on an outcrop of rock and went hurtling down the mountain-side. I passed the bearers carrying Mistress Elspeth and inquired her condition.

'We do not know, sir,' one of them answered, 'but we will carry her till we drop ourselves.'

At last I came up with John. He was choosing the route for the party and breaking the trail for it. His voice calling instructions and encouragement came back to me out of the darkness ahead, and it was not the mild voice I was accustomed to hearing him use. It was stern for all its encouragement, the tones those of a father who expects his children to obey him. It was the voice of authority I was hearing, the voice of a Chief. John must know his father was dead.

I stumbled forward to tread level with him and when we had exchanged greetings I told him what had happened in Inverrigan.

'Do you think they will follow us?' he asked.

'I think there is an even chance that the dissension between the officers will delay pursuit, at least,' I told him and he said,

'That is some comfort. We have lost thirteen of our party already, either dead or dying of exhaustion. We cannot move faster.'

'I went down to your father's house on my way up the glen,' I told him. 'You know what happened to him?'

He nodded. 'The young men I sent there brought the news to me.'

'And Lady Glencoe? Did they find her?'

'They found her body,' he said grimly. 'They told me—' He stopped, choking over the words and then, in a voice that rang like a cry of pain, he finished, 'They told me that the flesh of her fingers had been ripped off with her rings!'

I could find nothing to say, not even a word of comfort. I plodded on beside him for a few minutes longer and then I asked, 'How can I help? Tell me what you want me to do.'

'Take the child.' He turned and gestured to the nurse floundering along behind us with his baby son in her arms. 'She is weakening rapidly and my son is not safe with her now.'

I made to lift the baby from the woman. She held tight to it, glaring at me like a wild animal, and screamed. 'Would you deny me the honour of dying for my Chief's son!'

John laid his hand on her shoulder. 'Give him to Mr Stewart,' he commanded gently. 'He is young and strong and you are no longer fit to look after the child. And if I die—' He swayed suddenly, clutching at my shoulder. I steadied him, shocked to realize how far gone in exhaustion he was. 'If I die, nurse,' he finished, 'my son must survive to grow up as your Chief.'

Still the nurse hesitated, wailing protests at him. 'Obey me, woman!' he thundered at her, and with her voice rising in a crescendo of lamentation the woman handed the child to me. John moved forward to scale an outcrop of rock that stood some eight feet high in the way ahead of us. He stood at the top of it reaching his hand down to those who followed after. I wrapped the baby in the trailing shoulder-piece of my plaid, tied the end of it round me to leave my hands free, and climbed the rock to help John.

Together we tugged the young, the elderly and the infirm over the obstacle, and when the party was once more on the march John moved to the head of it again. An old man stumbling along with a boy of about six years appealed to me to help him, and I took the boy by the hand. The old man staggered along for another few minutes beside us, then quietly sank into the snow, and stayed motionless there for all my efforts to rouse him.

'Fourteen,' I muttered, desisting at last. And wondering how many more would die before we reached Glen Creran, I tucked the Chief's son firmly under my arm and dragged the older child on through the drifts with me.

The snow stopped falling around this time but the wind was still high. It blew the fallen snow in our faces, stinging them with showers of the powdery crystals. There was a general lightening of the sky above us which meant that daylight could not be far off, yet we were still climbing. We *had* to move faster, I thought, and the same compulsion must have struck John for he came along the line shortly afterwards, urging the people with voice and hands to move faster.

'Leave your dead, girl!' he ordered a young woman who had dropped to her knees and was keening bitterly over the body of another woman. He raised her to her feet and pushed her forward. 'Go, help the living!'

'Here, take this boy,' I told her. I unclasped the clinging hand of the small boy from mine and thrust him at her, then followed John back along the line and matched my efforts to his. We worked like demons to close the gaps in the long, straggling line, and on the far side of it we could hear Alasdair's voice as he ranged up and down with the same purpose. Soon, our combined efforts had awakened the younger men there from the lethargy the long, bitter struggle with the blizzard had induced in them, and burdened as they were with those too weak to walk alone, they still managed to quicken their pace.

John glanced round at the grey half-light of the winter's day growing in the sky and heaved a long sigh of relief.

'It will be full light in half an hour,' he said, 'but we shall have topped the last rise before that. You will see the waters of Loch Eilidh soon.'

I could not think of a more welcome sight for even the small weight of the baby I carried was now a burden that woke fresh aches in me with every step. My legs ached, my back ached. My head was stupid with fatigue and cold. I strained forward through the gusting snow for a sight of Loch Eilidh and when I saw the first steely shimmer of its waters in the dawn-light I could have wept with relief. We were over the top of the water-shed. In a few minutes we would be hidden from any pursuers and in under an hour we would be at Eilidh!

We began the downward slope to the loch and from that time the growing numbness in my mind increased till I was no longer acting consciously. I put one foot forward in front of the other but there was no intelligence guiding my steps. It was only the warmth of the child against me that kept a small flame of warning alight in my mind and when I stumbled, as I frequently did, I instinctively clasped the baby so that he would not be harmed if I fell.

In this state I arrived before my great-aunt's house at Eilidh. Our downward advance to the loch had apparently been noted by some of the servants for the doors of the house were open, the windows were alight, and figures came running forward to meet us. I saw Duncan the major-domo, advancing with hand out-stretched to John. A young girl whom I vaguely remembered as one of my great-aunt's dairy-maids appeared at my side, and with many exclamations of astonishment at my appearance took the baby from me.

Elizabeth met me at the door. She took me by the hand and I suffered her to lead me like a child towards the great fire blazing in the parlour. Wisely, she did not try to question me, but left me to lie where I had fallen in a stupor in front of the fire. The last thing I saw before my eyes closed was a swaying vision of many faces as a crowd of other survivors pressed round the fire. Then I slept.

The parlour was empty again when I awoke yet I had not slept long – less than three hours I guessed when I opened my eyes to see the hands on my great-aunt's elegant French time-piece showing only the half-hour after ten o'clock. I wondered where the survivors who had pressed into the parlour with me had gone, and was ashamed of myself for having fallen asleep when they had not apparently done so. Then I remembered that they must all have slept for at least a part of the previous night whereas I had not closed my eyes for a minute of it, and I felt less guilty.

My head throbbed. I sat up feeling it tenderly and heard Elizabeth's voice exclaiming 'Rob!' She had been sitting somewhere behind me waiting for me to wake, and when I stirred she came rushing forward to kneel at my side.

'My head, 'Lizbeth,' I groaned. 'Oh, my head!'

She embraced me, babbling foolish girl's talk in my ear, and though I was pleased to know her so glad to see me safe, I was still discomfited to be the subject of such a fuss. I broke away from her gently, so as not to hurt her feelings and asked:

'The Macdonalds? What has become of them all?'

'Some are still here at Eilidh,' she said, '—the sick, and those too elderly to go further. The others stayed only to rest for an hour and take some refreshment before they pressed on further down the glen with their Chief. His plan is to scatter them throughout various households in the glen so that they cannot be hunted down in a body if the red-coats come.'

'The Appin Stewarts will take this danger on themselves?' I asked.

'We at Eilidh have already done so,' she told me. 'The other households in Glen Creran will do the same for the sake of friendship and for hatred of the thing that has been done in Glencoe.'

I remembered Mistress Elspeth then and asked if she was still alive. Elizabeth looked sadly away from my question.

'She was dead when they carried her in at our door. The sword-thrust she got at Carnoch had pierced her lung.'

'So,' I said, 'you know everything that has happened?'

She nodded. 'John and Alasdair Og told it all.'

She looked at me biting her lip, and then she burst out with the questions she had been longing to ask me.

'Was Francis concerned in it, Rob? Did he rebel against the orders as you did? Where is he now? Tell me, please tell me!'

I got slowly to my feet and told her the little I knew about Francis. 'You must judge for yourself what he is likely to have done if he was given the kind of order that I refused to obey,' I added. 'If he acted like I did he will be like me now – on the run with capital charges hanging over his head. If he fell into line as the other officers did, he will be in Glencoe now, burning houses and looting Macdonald cattle – perhaps even dragging a few survivors from hiding to butcher them!'

'You must not talk like that about Francis!' she flared at me. 'He is an honourable man and a soldier – not a butcher!'

'So were the men of Glenlyon's troop till last night,' I said sourly, and regretted my tone immediately at the stricken look on her face.

'I am sorry, 'Lizabeth,' I said hastily, 'I do not know for certain that he was even in Glencoe last night. But supposing he was, any part he took in the massacre could still never be the crime committed by the troops who took Macdonald hospitality for a fortnight and then murdered their hosts. That is the true infamy of the massacre and it will rest on Glenlyon and his men till they die.'

'No! It will rest on their names also, long after they are dead!'

It was the voice of my uncle, Ian Stewart of Corbhain, which spoke from the doorway of the parlour. I swung round at the sound of it and saw him and my Great-Aunt Euphemia coming into the parlour. My uncle grasped me warmly by the hand, and my great-aunt rustled up to me and pecked at my cheek with withered lips.

'Y'are a great booby to get yourself in such a fix, Robert,' she observed. 'Nevertheless, you have preserved the name of Eilidh with honour, and we are proud of you. Are we not, Corbhain?'

'I would have thrashed him with my own hand if he had done less!' my uncle told her. He turned to me again. 'Yet you must be on your way quickly, Rob. There is no hiding-place in the West Highlands safe for you now!'

'But where can I go, sir?' I asked. 'Where in Scotland now could a rebel officer of the King hope to find safety!'

'We settled that while you were asleep, boy,' my great-aunt said briskly. 'I have written a letter for you to take to my very good friend the Duke of Gordon at his castle of Huntly, in Aberdeenshire. He will protect you from arrest for friendship's sake, and also because he is a staunch Jacobite. Moreover, he is the only Jacobite noble in Scotland powerful enough to shelter you in defiance of the Government! You will go east, therefore, to Huntly.'

'But Madam,' I protested, 'there are a hundred miles of mountains between here and Huntly! It would be an impossible feat to force a way through them under the present conditions of weather, yet there is no other way I could travel.'

'You can go by road, boy,' she retorted sharply. 'There is one that starts at the town of Spean Bridge, ten miles north-east of Fort William. It leads off the military road at Spean Bridge, bearing east at first and then taking a wide swing north-east. Follow it and you will come to Huntly.'

I stared in blank astonishment at this, for there is only one road from Glen Creran to Spean Bridge and that is the military one which runs along the southern bank of Loch Linnhe and then passes Fort William to continue by Spean Bridge through the Great Glen. How did she expect me to pass all the patrols that would be out on it now searching for survivors of the massacre, and the road-blocks that would have been set up to prevent them escaping from the west?

'Madam,' I protested again, 'I must take my chance of hiding in Appin with the rest of the survivors. There is no hope of going through the mountains to Huntly and I could never reach the road to it unseen by all the patrols that will be guarding the military road to Spean Bridge.'

'Do *not* presume to argue with me, Robert!' Glaring angrily at me she tapped her cane smartly on the floor.

'We do not yet know whether the military will pursue the Macdonalds into the mountains or whether they will be content simply to block any attempts they may make to escape from the west. The one thing we do know for certain is that they will have no mercy in hunting you down and Huntly is your best refuge. Therefore, *you will go to Huntly*!'

I turned to my uncle. 'Corbhain,' I appealed, 'pray speak for me! I will be arrested long before I reach Spean Bridge!'

He shook his head. 'You great-aunt is right, Robert, and you must do as she says. But you will not need to take the military road to Spean Bridge. Duncan will be going with you as your guide to Huntly and he will show you how to avoid it.'

He turned to Elizabeth. 'Miss, go see to some breakfast for your cousin.'

'And I,' said my great-aunt triumphantly, 'will send Duncan here with a better disguise for the boy than he is wearing just now. That Macdonald plaid he has on will only mark him out for pursuit!'

She swept out of the parlour after Elizabeth and I turned to my uncle impatient to hear how he proposed I should travel unseen to the meeting-point of the military road with the road to Huntly.

11 Flight

'The plan is a very simple one,' my uncle said. 'The military road to Spean Bridge runs along the south bank of Loch Linnhe and you can therefore make a detour round its route by crossing over to the northern bank of the loch and travelling up this till you come to the point where Loch Linnhe is joined by Loch Eil. You must then cross over Loch Eil by the neck of water called the Narrows and carry on to the village of Gairlochy. Bear east from Gairlochy for four miles and you will have completed a detour that will bring you out on to the Huntly road, one mile east of where it joins the military road at Spean Bridge.'

Duncan came in then carrying clothes of the sort a herd-boy would wear – a Stewart tartan plaid, a shirt of saffron yellow, a deerskin doublet, and brogans. He helped me to dress rapidly in these while my uncle went on with his explanation.

'Duncan will show you the quickest way from here to the road,' he told me, 'but once you are out of the shelter of our own Appin mountains you must travel only by night. And while you are secretly making your detour of the military road I will be riding openly along it to the farmhouse which stands at the point where you will strike the Huntly road. There is no reason why I should not travel thus boldly in daylight for the military do not know as yet that you are at Eilidh and so there is nothing to connect me with your escape from Glencoe.

'Towards dawn on your third night out of Eilidh, then, I will be waiting for you outside the farmhouse with your own Shadow and my best gelding, Black Boy. I will take anyone's wager that these are two of the fastest horses in the north, and once you are up in the saddle there is nothing can overtake you.'

He turned to Duncan. 'Remember, Duncan, they may have reasoned as we have done that he will be safest in the east. If they have, the countryside around Spean Bridge will be thick with patrols and the last few miles will be the most dangerous part of your journey.'

'What if we are seen and pursued at that point?' I asked. 'You will be in danger also if you are observed meeting us with the horses.'

My uncle laughed. 'I will be in no danger, I promise you! If you are seen at that point you must threaten me and pretend to steal the horses from me, and I will make sure that the farmer is there to be my witness and I was robbed of my horses by two unknown ruffians on the run from the red-coat patrol!'

I could think of no other objection to such a well-found plan and so I fell to rapidly on the porridge and cold mutton Elizabeth had brought in while we talked. While I ate I told my uncle briefly of what had passed between Glenlyon and myself concerning the Earl of Breadalbane and also of my other suspicions concerning the planning of the massacre. He made no comment on these, though his face grew very grim as he listened. I finished my meal and rose to take my leave of Eilidh.

'You will need a purse,' my uncle said when I had shaken hands with him. 'This coin should be sufficient for you.'

He handed a little leather bag which jingled as it passed between us. I thanked him for it and thrusting MacEachern's pistol into my belt I turned to Elizabeth and told her, 'Send me news of Francis if you can.'

She nodded, and I was not surprised to see that she was very close to tears. I was properly taken aback by my great-aunt's words of farewell, however, when I turned to her after embracing Elizabeth.

'Be sensible of your life, boy,' she said abruptly. 'I have a great tenderness for you and would see you alive again before my time is run out.'

I was too astonished by this at first to do more than murmur vaguely as I bent to kiss her hand. Then I looked up and was moved to see that she also was close to tears. In the first rush of affection I had ever felt for her I hugged her heartily and cried:

'I promise I will live to plague you yet, madam!' and with

that, I was away on the first stage of my attempt to escape from the west.

I stepped out of the house with Duncan into a day of white and blue and glittering gold. There was no wind. The white tops of the mountains were lined clear and sharp against a sky of brilliant, cloudless blue, and the sun sparkled in countless points of golden light over the snow. I looked out over the blinding white of it and found it difficult to believe that only a few miles away in Glencoe the same purity lay blackened by the smoking ruins of houses and trampled red with blood.

The throb of pain in my head vanished instantly in the clear air and even with only three hours sleep behind me I felt fresh and eager to move swiftly forward. Duncan set the pace, however, and he was cautious.

'Save your strength, Master Robert,' he advised. 'We have a long hard way to go from Glen Creran to the side of Loch Linnhe, and there will be a night's travel ahead of us still once we have reached the farther shore of the loch.'

He took the lead from me, breaking a trail up the ridge ahead of us with his long, slow mountaineer's stride. I fell in behind him, reluctantly at first, but it was not long before I saw the wisdom of his advice. The route he had chosen from Glen Creran lay over the high rock escarpment running down from the mountain of Sgorr a Choise, and then along Glen Duror to the loch-side. It was the shortest route out of the Appin mountains but it was also the most strenuous one, and we could not have covered it at my starting-pace without exhausting ourselves long before we reached the loch.

The sun had gone down and the shadows of the mountains had blotted the sparkle off the snow before Duncan called a halt. From the pack he carried on his back he drew bannocks and cheese for both of us, and pointing to the heathland stretching away from the widening mouth of Glen Duror he said:

'The military road runs over the moor ahead of us there. We will have to cross over it to reach the loch-side but we will wait till full dark before we do so.'

I nodded silent agreement. I was finding the bannock difficult to swallow and I was not sure if it was the dry oatmeal or fear that was sticking in my throat.

Duncan offered one more piece of information while we waited for full dark to gather in the sky. 'There has been a messenger sent ahead of us,' he said, 'to the boatman at the point of land called Rubha Mor. He will be waiting to ferry us across the loch.'

My uncle had considered everything, I thought, and then smiled as it occurred to me that it was perhaps my formidable great-aunt who had planned so carefully ahead. There was no more talk after that. We waited, huddled down with our plaids wrapped round us, till Duncan judged it was dark enough to start for the loch, then we set off across the moorland.

It was not truly full dark for the stars were brilliant that night. I was uneasily aware of the way they lit us, and in spite of myself I started in alarm when Duncan gripped my arm suddenly and whispered.

'We are near the road now. Get down and listen for a patrol.'

I sank down beside him hoping that from the road our crouching forms would look like any of the clumps of heather and gorse poking above the snow-covered moor around us.

'There will likely be road-blocks every mile along the way and soldiers patrolling between them the way it was in the rebellion,' Duncan's whisper continued. 'We must wait for a patrol to pass before we can be sure of crossing unseen.'

We had no choice but to do so, I thought. The ground on the far side of the road was flat and open and our figures moving over it would be visible for a considerable distance in the bright starlight. I strained to hear the sound of footsteps on the hard-packed snow of the road, but the night was cradled in silence.

We lay there unspeaking in the silence for almost an hour before we heard the first faint thud of footsteps. The sound grew in volume, and away to my right I saw a dark, moving mass appearing round a bend in the road. With a rhythmic marching tread that grew to a peak of sound and then faded away again, a patrol of twelve soldiers passed us. Duncan waited for at least ten minutes after the sound of their feet had died completely again, and then he touched my arm and whispered:

'Now!'

We jerked to our feet, ran across the road and, crouched low, kept on running across the flat ground on its farther side. Half a mile we covered like this before Duncan slowed to a walk. The ground in front of us had begun to slope downwards. I smelled the sea-weedy tang of Loch Linnhe's tidal water and saw the star-shot heave of them against the dark bulk of the Ardgour mountains on its farther shore.

Another half-mile's brisk walking brought us to the waterside. We plodded on, keeping to the snow-line just above the beach so that our footsteps would not ring on the shingle, and presently we heard a low whistle and saw the brief gleam of a lantern quickly flashed and then covered again.

We headed for it and made out the shape of a boat against the water. The figure of a man rose from the shingle as we approached. Duncan hailed him softly in Gaelic. The man answered in the same language, and when we came up to him he held the boat for us to climb aboard. Duncan took one oar, the boatman took the other and they pulled out over the loch. No further words were exchanged between them as they rowed the three miles to the farther shore, and rocked there on that great void of dark water between the mountains I had the sudden, strangest insight into what it felt like to be a native of a country under military occupation.

Tomorrow, the boatman might be questioned by a patrol, but if he knew nothing he could tell them nothing. Hence Duncan's silence and his own. Tomorrow the boatman would grin behind his hand as he saw red-coats keeping useless watch for me along the military road. Hence the waiting boat, the brief, dangerous gleam of the lantern and the long, hard pull to Loch Linnhe's northern shore. This, the unspeaking comradeship of the clans was the real strength of the Highlands, I thought, and was suddenly very aware of my Stewart blood and very proud of it.

Duncan took the lead again as soon as the boat grounded on the north bank of the loch, and we headed on northwards with the loch on our right and the mountains of Ardgour on our left. I had now been awake for nearly forty-eight hours with only two brief periods of rest and most of that time I had been actively on the move. Duncan's ordeal had lasted only half that time but he was more than three times my age. Our rate of walking dropped to a snail's pace after the first two miles and we stumbled often over our footing, but there was an equal stubbornness in us that kept us both on the move. It was only when we began lurching against one another like two men in wine that Duncan decided we must rest again.

He stopped and looked around, then pointed to the dark shape of a house a little way up the hillside on our left. 'It can only be an hour or so till daylight now,' he said. 'We had better beg shelter there.'

I followed him up the hillside wondering how we would be received, but I need not have troubled myself over that. Ardour is the territory of the McLeans, a clan that had been 'out' in the rebellion of 1688 and was friendly to the Stewarts. Within minutes of Duncan's knock and his explanation at the door we were seated by the fireside and the woman of the house was mixing oatmeal with hot water and honey and butter to make a bowl of brose. I supped down the hot, sweet stuff, content to let Duncan do the talking. It was all in the Gaelic, and though I understood nothing of it, it was clear from the horrified expressions of his hearers that he was telling of Glencoe.

Once we had eaten, they showed us to their own bed in one corner of the room. The woman chased away a gaggle of children who came clustering round us and sent one boy running down the hillside with a whispered message. The man reached up to the heather-thatch of the roof and drew out a broadsword and a pistol. He planted himself at the doorway, his figure outlined against the faint dawn light, and Duncan said to me:

'Sleep now, and we will travel as soon as it is dark again. Meanwhile, he will not let us be taken by surprise.'

So began the pattern of the next two days and nights of our flight. We now travelled only by night to lessen the risk of meeting with any of the Outpost Patrols which made occasional sweeps beyond the Fort's direct area of command, and by day we rested in a friendly household.

No one turned us away. No one hesitated, even in the face

of the dreadful fate of the Macdonalds, to give us shelter. Each dawn our story was received with a silent horror that said more than any anger or lamentation could have done. Each dawn the woman of the house gave us food and bed while the man of the house took down his weapons and stood guard while we slept. And from each household, I noticed, a child was sent running with the word of who we were and what had happened in Glencoe.

That word would be spread all through the mountains of Ardgour, Duncan told me. We were still only two against the nearly nine hundred men in Fort William but now, if we had to run into the mountains in front of a patrol, there would be an army of grim-faced McLean men waiting there to cover our escape with the swords and pistols that had been hidden in the thatch of their houses since the end of the rebellion.

On the third night, we began on the last and most dangerous stage of our journey. Passing Fort William with its sentry-light gleaming faintly at us from the opposite shore of Loch Linnhe we bore left for the Narrows of Loch Eil, and here we encountered our first check. Our host of the previous day had arranged for us to be ferried over the Narrows, but the boat-man was late at the rendezvous. When he did come, an hour later than we expected to meet him, he brought bad news with him.

'I have been stopped by a patrol and held for questioning,' he told us. 'If you are headed for Gairlochy, sirs, you had better keep well up the slope of Meall Bhanabhie to the left of the track there. The red-coats have been patrolling it this past two days and they have road-blocks set up at Gairlochy itself, as well.'

His advice only confirmed my uncle's warnings on the danger of this part of our journey, but we heard it with the greater dismay since we had already lost time in waiting for him and would lose more through the detour he recommended. How much time, we could only guess, but we could not afford to be late at the rendezvous with my uncle for he would not dare to linger there. He would certainly fall under suspicion from the troops at Spean Bridge if he did so and would be held for questioning by the officer in charge. If that happened we would have to postpone our attempt to meet him till darkness fell again, and to hide for the whole of the intervening day in such a closely-patrolled area would increase ten-fold our chances of being caught.

We set off at our best pace accordingly, and kept this up till we were level with the village of Gairlochy. We could see the gleam of the lanterns on the road-blocks at either end of the village from where we stood on the slope of Meall Bhanabhie, and we swung round them in a wide circle towards the River Lochy. We reached it safely but it had taken us much longer to do so than we expected, and we lost even more time in casting up and down the river for a suitable place to cross.

Time was now our enemy as much as the patrols. We estimated that we had just over an hour of darkness left to us when we reached the farther bank of the river and this was barely enough for our purpose.

There were still four miles of heathland between us and the rendezvous on the Huntly road – four miles of open ground on which we could be surprised at any moment. Moreover, the military road from which we had curved away at Rubha Mor cuts straight across this heath on its way to Spean Bridge, and to reach the farther side of the town we would have to cross over this road again. We held a quick consultation on the hazards involved, and deciding that it would be better to take the lesser chance of being caught on this last four miles than the greater one of hiding for another day before we tried to break out, we set off running across the moor.

We did not throw caution entirely aside – Duncan was too old and wily and my military training was too fresh in my mind to allow of that. The heath was broken by ridges and hillocks of higher ground, and we were careful not to let ourselves be seen against the skyline when we crossed these higher points. And once over the crest of a ridge, we carefully spied the open ground ahead for any movement before we descended to run quickly for the next ridge.

So must many a rebel clansman have fled with rapid caution before my own approach in command of an Outpost Patrol, I thought, and found myself almost enjoying the grim humour of the situation!

We reached the military road without mishap, however, and crouched down among a tumble of rocks beside it. These gave us reasonable cover for the moment but there was even better cover on the far side of the road for the ground there took a dip which would hide us almost immediately from the view of any approaching patrol. Nor could we afford to wait till the next patrol due had passed our hiding-place. In a few minutes we would be seen as dark shadows against grey. Very soon after that there would be enough light to show us clearly. We held another brief conference and decided on an immediate crossing of the road.

Like hares bolting for a form we dashed to the other side of the road and down into the dip of ground beyond it. We landed in bog, our feet cracking sharply through the skin of ice which lay under its coating of snow. I sank over the ankles in icy water. Duncan, being heavier than I, sank almost to the knees. I reached a hand to him, shouting to him to grip it, and linked like this we struggled forward. There was no telling where the bog ended since the snow that lay over everything concealed its limits. There was a shoulder of rising ground on our left, however, and we floundered slowly towards this.

A hundred yards farther on we reached firm ground again, but that short distance had cost us dear in time. The sky above us held the pearly glow of pre-dawn light and in the eastern sky ahead there was already a faint wash of yellow colour. We could see Spean Bridge as a huddle of dark roofs below us in the valley on our right and knew that with little more than a mile to go we still could not be at the rendezvous before daybreak.

We rounded the shoulder of rising ground beyond the bog and saw the contour of the last mile we would have to cover on foot. It stretched level ahead of us for a quarter of that distance before it began dropping down towards the Huntly road, and on our left rose a ridge of fairly steep, rocky ground. Duncan watched ahead towards the road as we went, with an occasional glance down at Spean Bridge on his right, but it was the rock-ridge on our left which occupied my attention.

If *I* were charged with guarding the junction of the military road with the road to Huntly, I thought, that was where I would station my men. From that steep ridge I could keep not only the junction of the two roads in view but all the approaches to them also. From there, at this very moment, there was now light enough to pick us out clearly against the snow-covered heath.

I drew Duncan's attention to the dangers of the ridge and we strode on for the next few hundred yards with our heads turned watchfully towards it. The end of it came in sight and Duncan said,

'I doubt you are wrong, Master Robert. There is—'

A shot rang out from the ridge. It carried Duncan's bonnet away with it and he flung himself face downwards in the snow, one arm across my shoulders taking me with him. I jerked myself free of his weight and craned my head up towards the ridge. It was alive with red-coated figures appearing from its rocky folds. They stood still with muskets levelled, except for one man who waved and shouted to us to stay where we were.

The shot had been a warning one, I realized, and decided that it must have been simply luck which had brought it so close to us. We were well within musket-range certainly, but our soldiers had not been trained to take more than a general aim when they fired. Their musket-practice had all been directed to firing rapid vollies at a massed, stationary target and none of them could have been expected to hit a moving figure at that distance. Sergeant Barbour was the only man in the Regiment with enough skill in musketry for such a feat, but there was no way of telling as yet whether it was he who had fired the warning shot.

Some of the soldiers began on their way down the ridge. We scrambled to our feet but as soon as we moved there was a volley of musket-fire. Duncan would have gone down again but I grasped his arm and urged him on with me. If it *was* Barbour in charge of this patrol I knew exactly how many seconds we had before the next volley was fired. I counted our steps aloud to the order of the numbers in his musket-drill and dropped down dragging Duncan with me at the second I imagined the order *'Present!'* would come, immediately before the final command of *'Fire!'*

My count had been exactly right for Barbour's timing. The second volley rang out as we hit the ground and I knew then that it must be he who was in command, for with any other Sergeant there would have been a longer gap between the first and second vollies. Still counting I was up again, waving Duncan on with me. He had grasped the meaning of my counting by this time. He watched me as he ran, and not the soldiers, and was ready to drop with me ahead of the next volley.

I watched the soldiers. We would be out of the range of fire soon if there was no change in their tactics, yet we had declared our rebel status by running from them and I could not believe that Barbour would allow two such obvious fugitives to escape him.

He would try to head us off, I guessed, and I was right. A number of soldiers broke away from the main body and ran for the end of the ridge. They kept on beyond the point where it sloped down into the flat ground of the heathland, and all except four of them began to fan out in a wide, encircling movement. The group of four kept close together and ran in line with us.

I pointed to this group. 'Watch these four!'

Duncan nodded. 'Aye. We can out-run the others.'

He was panting, but he was still running easily and so was I – far more easily than the soldiers trying to head us off. We had the advantage of them with our light brogans and free-swinging plaids compared to their heavy boots and cumbersome uniform coats.

We kept our eyes on this group of four and saw them come to a sudden halt. One swung a musket up, steadied it on the shoulder of another of the group, and fired. The shot whistled close to us, close enough to tell me it must be Barbour who was firing, but not close enough to stop us running. The next shot would be the dangerous one – the one that would come when he had steadied his breathing sufficiently to take really accurate aim.

We dropped together as it rang out and kicked a wild flurry

in the snow a few inches from my left hand. More shots followed in quick succession, spurting the snow around us. One went through my plaid at the shoulder. Another nicked Duncan's ear. I counted six shots fired at even intervals and guessed that the speed of their firing meant that Barbour had brought the three other men with him to act as loaders while he fired.

We would be safer running than lying there as a target for his sharp-shooting, I thought, and at the shot that grazed his ear Duncan spoke the same thought aloud. Besides, the longer Barbour could pin us there the more time his circle of men would have to close in on us.

Once again, we sprang to our feet and ran. This time we did not keep a straight course but ran in a series of swerves that we hoped would upset Barbour's aim, and this succeeded to some extent for his shots began to fall wider of us. We were adding to the distance we would have to run to outpace the cordon, of course, and knowing this we summoned our last burst of speed.

Barbour's firing stopped. I glanced quickly back and saw that he and his loaders had begun running again in an effort to reduce the range of fire. The leader in the line of circling men was now ahead of us but there was a considerable gap between him and the man following him. We headed in a diagonal line for this gap. The leading runner stopped as we changed direction, shouldered his musket and fired. The second man fired also, but both shots went wide. We ran on while they re-loaded, running straight into their line of fire.

Their muskets cracked within a second of one another as we ran through the gap between them. I felt a numbing blow on my right forearm and thought a ball must have pierced it, but it had only been grazed. Duncan passed through the cross-fire unscathed and steadied my momentary stumble as the bullet struck me.

We could see the line of the road ahead of us now and by the side of it the squat outline of the farmhouse where my uncle should be waiting with the horses. Behind us the soldiers were still firing, single shots that came at irregular intervals and fell wide, but Barbour was still pursuing. If my uncle was not at the rendezvous we could not hope to escape his next burst of shooting.

A smooth slope of snow led downward to the road. It was steep, and I could see ourselves tumbling headlong if we tried to run down it at our present pace, but Duncan pointed to it and gasped out:

'There is scree under that snow. Throw yourself down and slide!'

We reached the slope. Duncan dashed the first few yards down it, dug his heels in and let himself fall sideways. I copied his example and found myself shooting down the slope in a rattle of small stones and snow. We rolled head over heels at the foot of it, picked ourselves up at a bound and ran on without pause. Away above us the red-coats were treading cautiously down the loose, sliding rock of the scree-slope, not daring the wild glissade which had allowed us to enlarge our lead on them.

Fifty yards up the road two men stood watching the scene. One was my uncle, holding Black Boy and Shadow by the reins, and I guessed that the other must be the farmer. They were talking excitedly together and the farmer was pointing to the red-coats above us.

'Fire at them,' Duncan gasped. 'Fire wide!'

We drew our pistols and fired. The farmer turned and ran for the safety of his house. My uncle stood his ground, shouting and shaking his fist at us. We shouted back with what breath we had and rushed up to him brandishing our empty pistols. Duncan snatched the reins. I leapt on my uncle, bearing him back into the snow.

'Ride hard, and God go with you,' he muttered, and lay still where I had thrown him.

Duncan was in Black Boy's saddle as I rose. He tossed Shadow's reins to me and I was on the grey's back in one bound. We put our mounts to the road at a gallop, bending low in the saddle while one musket-shot after another whined over our heads.

I risked a backward glance. My uncle had staggered to his feet and was standing in the middle of the road, his pistol raised to fire. The shot came and fell well to our right. The soldiers kept on firing but all their shots fell wide also, except for one. A lucky one, or one of Barbour's, I thought, and addressed all my attention to keeping Shadow at a gallop along the road to Huntly.

12 Escape into darkness

It was not a road at all, properly speaking, but simply a broad track beaten out by the passage of cattle-herds to the south. The snow over-lying its stony surface made it all the more dangerous for swift riding, but with musket-shots falling all round us we had no choice except to sacrifice caution for speed.

We rode hard as my uncle had bidden, therefore, and the fear that Barbour might commandeer horses from the farmer to pursue us kept us on at the gallop well after we were out of musket range. Both Shadow and Black Boy rose gallantly to the challenge of the effort we called from them, and it was only when they had come to the end of their first wind that we reined in and allowed them to drop to a canter and then a trot.

There were four days of rough travel ahead of us, Duncan warned me then, but I did not mind this for I knew that if we could only maintain a pace fast enough to keep ahead of pursuit for the first day, our escape would have succeeded. Barbour could only hope to find mounts quickly for a few men, after all, and however vindictive he was Barbour was also too good a soldier to venture more than a day's ride into hostile territory without adequate forces to back him.

Our way lay by Kingussie, Grantown-on-Spey and Keith to Huntly, with the Cairngorm mountain range on our right and the Monadhliath Mountains on our left – a difficult journey in winter but not a dangerous one from the point of pursuit since we were bearing away all the time from the western garrison of Fort William and the one north-east of it at Inverness. The weather and our own fatigue, Duncan remarked as he described the route to me, would be the worst enemies we would have to combat.

By the time we had been ten hours in the saddle, riding hard all the time, I was in full agreement with him. The short winter day had ended with no sight or sound of pursuit behind us and I reckoned it was both high time we called a halt for rest and safe enough to do so. We were well into a long stretch of moor, however, with no sign of human habitation on it. I was at a loss to know how we would pass the night but Duncan took our situation in his stride.

'There is no Highlander yet ever came to harm from a night in the snow, Master Robert,' he said cheerfully. 'We will do as the clansmen do when they are out on a raid in winter and night overtakes them.'

He swung off his horse and first of all shared out more of our bannocks and cheese before he turned to making a firm, man-length hollow in the snow.

'Now,' he instructed me, 'do likewise for yourself, and when you have made the hollow lie down in it with your plaid wrapped – so!'

Lying down in the hollow he had made he wrapped the shoulder-piece of his plaid round his upper body and pulled a loose fold of the material up over his head. I copied his example as best I could and lowered myself down into my snow-hollow.

It was like lowering myself into a grave! I shuddered with horror at the feeling and at the touch of the cold snow against my bare legs, but soon I was surprised to feel drowsiness creeping over me. The plaid close-wrapped round me had begun to form a cocoon of warmth within the narrow space in which I lay, and before many more minutes were past my drowsiness had grown to the point where I drifted off to sleep.

I found myself back in Glencoe in the dreams which troubled my sleep. Glenlyon's tall form came stalking to me out of the snow and fixed me motionless before the glittering, manic gaze of its eyes. I pulled MacEachern's pistol and shot at him. The shot made no sound in my dream and Glenlyon's form vanished in the dissolving smoke of it. In his place there rose up the young huntsman I had saved from the stag and the little boy with his Book of Tales. They stood hand in hand looking reproachfully at me and I shouted to them telling them to run but no sound came from my mouth, and suddenly Duncanson and Drummond were there also, one on either side of me, and the huntsman was sinking to his knees with a bullet-hole in his forehead and the little boy was screaming as Drummond's dagger pierced his neck.

I tried to run from the sight but my feet weighed so heavily I could scarcely move them. The snow came down in a heavy white curtain before my eyes and through the curtain came drifting the form of Lady Glencoe with her hands held cupped in front of her.

'Have you seen my rings, Mr Stewart?' she asked me. 'I have been searching everywhere for my rings, but all I could find was this.'

She held out her hands to me. The blood dripped from her mutilated fingers on to the snow and in her cupped palms I saw the tiny, curved fingers of a baby's hand. Then the snow swept down on me again and blotted her from my sight. I struggled to force a way through it, brushing the beating flakes madly aside with both hands. The strong fingers of some unseen person gripped my shoulder and I tried to break away from them. I had to run! I had to escape . . . I must escape . . .

I shouted the words aloud and woke suddenly to find Duncan shaking me by the shoulder and the snow falling heavily on my face. 'We must be moving, Master Robert,' Duncan was saying. 'Daylight will be on us soon.' I shook the mists of nightmare from my brain and rose to follow him wondering how I could endure another three such days and nights before we reached Huntly.

That second day of our journey was little different from the first. We did not push the horses quite so hard, but once again we had to sleep in the open, and once again Glencoe haunted my sleep. On our third night we were more fortunate and were able to shelter in a hostelry in the town of Carrbridge. My dreams that night were less fearsome but by now I had reached the stage where I could not put Glencoe out of my waking thoughts, and all through the third and fourth days of our ride I brooded on every aspect of it.

Duncan tried to rouse me from my gloom by talking about our route, pointing out the peaks towering on either side of us and naming them for me, but I was too sunk in my own thoughts to heed him. It was only when we were on the last few miles of our journey towards evening on our fourth day that I began to think ahead to my meeting with the Duke of Gordon. I had no desire to appear before this gentleman in my present beggarly condition, my hair all matted and my clothes and person filthy. When I told Duncan so he patted the saddle-bags carried by Black Boy and told me cheerfully:

'Your great-aunt thought of that! There is clean linen and a change of clothes for you in these bags. You can make your toilet in the Gordon Arms in the village of Huntly and I will take your letter to the Duke while you do so. His castle is only half a mile from the village.'

We rode down the last mile of the little valley that led to Huntly and dismounted beside the market cross in the village square. The Gordon Arms faced us on one side of the square. Duncan took the saddle-bags and led the way into it, shouting for a groom to take our horses. Two servants appeared and he left me with one of them while he went off with the other to attend to the horses before going up to the castle.

I tossed the bags to the other fellow and bade him show me a room where I could wash and change my clothes, and within a few minutes was stripping off my Stewart plaid in front of a fire while he ran to fetch a tub and hot water for me.

Impatiently I waited for the tub to be prepared and as soon as the fellow had finished tipping the water into it I chased him from the room and turned to the pleasure of soaking a week's dirt from my skin. Clean and dressed again as befitted my station, I thought as I splashed, I would have the confidence to present my case sensibly to the Duke, and when my tubbing was over I reached contentedly for the saddlebags.

From one I drew some of the clean linen that filled it and put this on. Then I reached inside the other one and the first thing my hand encountered was a letter addressed to me in Elizabeth's hand. I broke the seal on it and read,

To my dear cousin Robert, pray not to be angry with me. Great-Aunt Euphemia bade me pack your clothes and I have put in the uniform you left with her for mending some months ago. There is a cloak also which will cover its colour when you go abroad. Pray forgive me, Robert! I did this because I know your heart is so set on soldiering that you will not be happy without a uniform on your back and because I feel there still must surely be an opportunity for you some time to resume your service. Also, pray do not let Great-Aunt know it was your uniform I packed or she

will whip me, for you know she is so ardent in the Jacobite
cause that she greatly dislikes to have you wear the King's coat.
And I will pray for you, dear coz.

Elizabeth

I dropped the letter, and pulling my red uniform coat from the saddle-bag I stood unhappily with it in my hand for several moments. It was my second-best uniform, the double of the one I had left behind me in Glen Muidhe except for the tear in the sleeve where I had caught it on a rack of halberds in the Fort's armoury. The tear had been so neatly mended that it was almost invisible now. I smoothed the darn with my finger and thought that a cloak would be all very fine for cover when I went abroad – but what of all the people who might see me within walls and wonder what a red-coat officer was doing in the heart of the Jacobite territory of Huntly?

I had every cause to be angry with Elizabeth for her foolishness in sending the uniform, I thought, but it was a more complicated feeling than fear of discovery that was making me hesitate with it in my hand. I was not sure that I wanted to take King William's coat on my back again now that I had had time to think deeply about Glencoe! It was he who had given the order for the massacre, after all. The order paper had read, *'This is by the King's special commands.'*

And yet – I had always before heard King William spoken of as an honourable man! My father had served under his personal command and he had described him to me as a man of reserved nature but very fair in his judgments and asking no more of any soldier than he was willing to perform himself. Could it really have been he who had ordered old men and babies to be murdered in their beds? Could such a man have planned the terrible act of treachery which had apparently been the vital factor for success in the whole design of the massacre?

Uneasily, as I fingered the coat, I wondered if I had any right to judge King William till I knew the answers to these questions. My hope of future service in his army lay buried deep under the snow in Glen Muidhe, but had I any right to dig a grave for my oath of loyalty also till I knew more of his blood-guilt for Glencoe? It was only my court-martial which could provide the answers to all these questions, I decided, and until that took place I still had the duty as well as the right to wear the King's coat on my back.

Quickly on the decision, I slipped it on. It was a smart coat. The cut of it sat easily on my shoulders and the familiar feel of it was curiously comforting after a week of wearing a plaid. With great satisfaction I settled myself into it and a few minutes later I had finished dressing. I called the servant and paid him, then for fear they could cause questioning I bundled my discarded clothes into one of the saddle-bags, and sat down to wait for Duncan's return.

He was a long time in coming. As I waited I grew angry and uneasy by the minute at his tardiness, but when he arrived eventually he was smiling.

'Quickly, Master Robert!' he told me, and without giving me a chance to question him he swept up the saddle-bags and hurried out of the room. I followed him, expecting him to rush out for the horses, but instead of doing so he led me to another room in the inn, threw open the door and beckoned me to enter. I did so, full of curiosity to know what I would find there and came face to face with a man standing before the peat fire on the hearth.

He was dressed in a very fine jacket of dark green velvet laced with silver and tartan trews patterned with the same dark green, but the fire and a single candle were all the light in the room and this was all I had opportunity to note about him before Duncan said:

'Here he is, Your Grace,' and then, turning to me, 'Master Robert, please to make the acquaintance of the Duke of Gordon.'

I bowed, too confused by the suddenness of the encounter to look more closely at the man. Then, as I glanced up, I received a swift impression of a dark, haughty face, very firm and determined-looking above the silver lacing of his coat.

'Sir, I judged it wiser for me to come here than for you to come to the castle,' the Duke said. 'Servants can be indiscreet – even the most loyal of servants.'

He gestured me to a chair. 'Pray sit, Mr Stewart. I dislike your uniform but I have an admiration for your great-aunt and I like what she says about you in her letter. Nevertheless, I require to hear your story from your own lips. Pray therefore begin, and leave out nothing in the telling that might have a bearing on this affair.'

I sat down on the chair he had indicated and considered where I should begin my story. For me at least, I decided, the affair of Glencoe had started with MacIan's visit to the Fort on that wild December night when I had held the watch at the Spur Gate, and so I began my story from there. The Duke listened attentively all the time I spoke, his head bent and turned away from me so that I could not judge his thoughts from the expression on his face.

When I had finished he paced the room for several minutes and then he said sharply, 'Mr Stewart, regarding your account of the correspondence between Lieutenant Colonel Hamilton and Stair, the Secretary of State – are you quite sure the lieutenant who spoke of it to your friend, Farquhar, is a truthful man?'

'Gil Kennedy would not lie, sir, I'll swear to that,' I answered, 'and he is too sensible to have been mistaken over it.'

'And you have also told me exactly what passed between you and Alasdair Og MacIan, and you and Glenlyon, concerning my lord Breadalbane?'

'I have given it to you word for word, sir.'

'Very well. Very well.'

Once again the Duke paced the room in silence, then abruptly he came to a decision.

'I believe your story, Mr Stewart,' he told me, 'therefore I will offer you sanctuary and protection for as long as you need it. But not in my castle, since that is too public a place for one in your situation. There is a lodge not far from it where you can be both private and safe, for I will put an armed guard of my own men round it day and night. My servants are outside. They will take you to it and you must lie there till you receive word from your friends in Appin that it is safe to venture forth again.'

Without giving me time to thank him he strode to the door, and then turned there to consider me for a moment.

'You may comfort yourself in hiding, Mr Stewart,' he said, 'with the thought that this matter is not ended. The secret of the massacre escaped from Appin with you, and I can assure you it will not be long before the whole country knows of it and cries for vengeance on those responsible.'

Then he was gone. Duncan said, 'I will fetch the horses,' and followed him out. I waited a few minutes then went outside and found him waiting for me.

Two men in the green tartan of the Gordons were with him. They ran ahead of us along a narrow street that led out of the square and on to a track through the woodland lying beyond it. I heard hooves thudding away to my left as we followed the Gordon men and guessed it was the Duke riding back to his castle, and presently I glimpsed the great red-stone pile of it in a hollow to that side of the woodland. Our guides bore still farther to the right of it and presently we came out into a clearing with a small, stone-built lodge at the centre of it.

There was a light in one window of the lodge and a woman answered to our guide's knock on the door. Duncan followed the Gaelic of her conversation with them and told me:

'She is wife to the Duke's head forester. They are telling her of the plans the Duke has made for you. You will be comfortable here, Master Robert, and perfectly safe at last.'

It was at that moment I realized that I no longer thought of Duncan as a servant. He was indeed as much a Stewart of Eilidh as I was, and he had been a staunch friend to me. I owed him much, I thought gratefully – and if anyone had told me at that moment that I would find his promised safety tedious beyond endurance I would have laughed in their face!

Yet so it happened. I ate good cooked food that evening and I slept that night in a comfortable bed. In the morning I took a warm farewell of Duncan, and then began the most miserable six weeks of my life.

The Duke more than kept his word about guarding me. Over and above the armed men who stood always at the door of the lodge it seemed to me that wherever I looked I saw men in the green Gordon tartan keeping watchful eyes on me.

Indeed, it was like being watched by the very landscape itself so quietly did they follow me, so still they blended into the background when I stopped and turned to catch a sight of them.

Gradually, however, I learned to ignore their presence. Gradually the feeling of irritation at being constantly watched yielded to a dull acceptance of the security provided by such careful surveillance, and by the time the month of March was half-over I had come to take that security entirely for granted.

I had been four weeks in hiding by that time and I was so sick of it that I would willingly have exchanged my safety for the dangers of Appin again. I saw nothing more of the Duke of Gordon and when I inquired about him I was told that he had ridden to Edinburgh on the day after my arrival at Huntly. I had no conversation with anyone, therefore, and so I had recourse to interminable games against myself with the chess set His Grace had instructed to be sent to me from the castle, and when I was tired of this I taught the head forester the game.

I drew out the plans of a hundred battles and pursued them on paper with phantom troops against imagined hazards. And as darkness fell each day I cloaked the red of my uniform coat and slipped out to the stables where the head forester had Shadow saddled up for me. Once up on his back and away through the darkness I had a brief illusion of freedom, but always, however far and fast I rode I heard behind me the hoof-beats of my guards' horses, and despairingly knew myself the prisoner of a safety I had come to hate.

I took to standing for long stretches at a time gazing out of my window in the hope of seeing Duncan returning with the letters he had promised to bring me from Eilidh, but day after day passed without a sight of him. March was into its third week before he arrived and I fell on him eagerly with the questions fairly tumbling from me.

I was especially curious to know whether it had in fact been Barbour who had pursued us to the Huntly road, and whether he had followed us along it.

Duncan's face lit up with sardonic glee when I asked him about this and he said, 'Oh, aye, you were right enough about

Barbour being the one in charge of that patrol. And he did pursue us – but not for long. The horses he took from the farmer to follow us were never meant for hard galloping and the poor beasts foundered before he had ridden them half a day – and now the farmer has put in a claim for damages to Colonel Hill!'

I laughed with him over this but Duncan's face grew quickly solemn again and he added:

'There is a darker side to the tale, though, Master Robert, for Barbour has convinced himself and everyone else that it must have been you who ran from him at Spean Bridge. No one except an officer, he maintains, would have had the knowledge to use the timing of his own musket-drill against him the way you did.'

Dismayed, I asked, 'But do they know where I am now?'

Duncan handed me two letters. 'Read these,' he told me. ' 'Tis all there in them.'

I broke the seal of one in my uncle's hand and read,

This is to warn you, Rob, to stay close where you are for they know you are out of Appin but do not yet know where you are hiding. There is a proclamation of arrest against you posted throughout all the West Highlands, and the word is that there is great confusion at the Fort over the bungling of the massacre through the fault of the blizzard and the warnings you gave – also through warning given by the common soldiery who misliked the task they were given to do. I hear that Lt Colonel Hamilton is now in disfavour over this bungling and that Col Hill fears a massed rising of the clans in anger against the treatment of the Macdonalds. He also fears ambush of his troops from clan-allies of Glencoe if he sends to pursue the Macdonalds into the mountains. They are therefore being left unmolested in Appin meantime, and until Col Hill has further instructions from London he is contenting himself with containing the west with road-blocks and patrols so that none can enter or leave it without answering to the military. We have taken a count of the Macdonalds in hiding, both those who escaped with you through Glen Muidhe and others who managed to climb through the passes of the Lairig Gartain and the Lairig Eilde, and find that seventy-eight people in all are missing – either killed in the massacre or died attempting to escape. Maclean's sons are very strenuous in looking after their people and send you hearty thanks for your help of them. Alasdair is very low in spirits over his wife's death but sends also to tell you that some of the huntsmen of the clan made an escape over the mountain of Sgor na Ciche, into Mamore. This being a climb few would dare even in the best of weather conditions and you having hunted with these young men, he tells me you would wish to know of their remarkable escape.

Seventy-eight people dead – nearly a fifth of the clan! It was a far cry, of course, from the complete massacre that had been envisaged but it was still an appalling toll of lives. Yet it was cheering to know I had been right to hope that not all the common soldiery would consent to take part in the butchery! And as for the climb of the huntsmen over Sgor na Ciche – I thought of the sheer sides of the great conical peak guarding the entrance to the glen and the force of the wind that must have plucked at them as they climbed, and could find no words to express my admiration for such a feat!

I turned to my second letter, which was from Elizabeth. It was much longer and more rambling than my uncle's one but it contained little else in the way of news except for one short paragraph which read:

We have not been able to discover anything about Francis except that he is no longer at Fort William. I greatly fear for him. If he was in Glencoe and rebelled as you did he cannot have been so lucky in his escape as you or he would surely have let me know his whereabouts by this time.

But had I in fact, been so lucky? I brooded over this question once Duncan had taken his departure again with my own letters in reply to these two, and could not find an answer to it. True, I was still alive in freedom of a kind but what sort of prospect did the future hold out for me?

I wore the King's coat on my back but I would never fight in King William's army again. I could take service abroad, perhaps, but was there any army which would give a commission to an officer with my record of rebellion and desertion? I could serve as a private gentleman volunteer in some foreign army, of course, but that would be a poor substitute for all the glorious dreams I had dreamed of a military career. Gentleman volunteers did not command strategy. They had no opportunity to practise the science of war.

There was no more future for me as a soldier, yet there was no other occupation in which I could be happy. In Glencoe, watching the time creep on towards the moment of massacre, I had faced this prospect and accepted it as my duty. But now I had had time to savour the reality of it and the taste was more bitter in my mouth than I had ever dreamed it would be.

I grew very dull and listless in the next two weeks. With nothing to beckon me forward to the future my mind turned constantly back to Glencoe. I thought often of MacEachern and the brave, stupid way he had died, and when I said prayers for his soul I almost wished it had been myself who had fallen to Glenlyon's pistol that night.

I was no longer alert when I rode out on Shadow. I no longer kept MacEachern's pistol freshly primed in my belt by day or under my pillow at night. There seemed no point in doing so. Indeed, so low in spirits was I that there seemed no point in anything at all to me any more – and certainly not in troubling to take precautions against being surprised by a patrol of red-coats. My Gordons were there to protect me against that possibility, and with the close guard they kept on me such a situation could never arise.

The shock that travelled through me, therefore, when I looked from my window one day at the end of March and saw three men in red coats riding up to the lodge, was so violent that for several seconds I was held transfixed and helpless before the sight.

13 The King's order

Suddenly, life still seemed a sweet thing to have!

I snatched MacEachern's pistol from my belt and hurriedly primed it. There was a back entrance to the lodge and if I could slip out of this I would be able to reach the stables and be up on Shadow and away before my pursuers could reach the front door. My hands shook over the priming and I cursed both my guards and my own lassitude in the past two weeks.

I cocked the pistol and flung a last glance out of the window to judge the time I had left to reach the stables. The red-coats were very close – not more than fifty yards away. And they were not alone!

Bewildered I checked, still half-poised for flight, and stared out of the window. There were two of my Gordon men trotting alongside the red-coats' horses and one of them looked very much like the man who had command of my guards. Had the Duke, then, decided to give me up to this patrol? If he had, there was no point in my running for my only hope of completing such an escape would lie in the friendly help his clan might give me.

I stood torn with painful indecision. The soldiers were nearer now. I could see that the two in the lead were officers and the one riding behind them was a trooper. There was something familiar about the appearance of the officers . . .

I waited, keeping the pistol cocked and pointed at the door of the room. The horses clattered to a halt outside the lodge. Vocies reached me, then the sound of footsteps which grew louder and louder till they halted outside my door. The door opened and framed in it I saw Major John Forbes and Lieutenant Francis Farquhar. Their eyes met mine for a flash before their gaze dropped to the pistol in my hand.

'Put down that pistol, Ensign Stewart,' Forbes snapped.

He came towards me and I backed away from him keeping the pistol levelled at his heart.

'Keep your distance I beg, sir,' I said hoarsely. 'I do not want to kill you, but—'

I backed from him again but still he came towards me. When I could go no further he halted also, and with only a few feet now separating us he held out his hand to me, palm upwards.

'Give me the pistol,' he commanded.

'Robert!' Francis Farquhar called urgently from the doorway. 'The Major has not come to arrest you!'

Forbes kept his eyes unwaveringly fixed on mine. He was not at all afraid of the pistol, I realized, and suddenly I felt a fool for having threatened him with it. Forbes was a just officer and a humane man. As for Francis – he had been my friend once. And yet . . . and yet . . . I was a fugitive from all these two men represented. The pistol had cost me very dear to obtain and it was now my only defence against sudden trickery on their part.

Slowly, very slowly I let my hand drop, and ignoring the Major's one outstretched to me, I thrust the pistol back into my belt.

'I accept the compromise, Ensign Stewart,' Major Forbes said gravely.

My voice trembling in spite of myself I asked them, 'If you have not come to arrest me, sir, what do you want of me? And how did you find me?'

'Your great-aunt told me where you had hidden yourself – once I had managed to convince her with solemn oaths that you would come to no harm if she did so. And as to what I want – I see you still wear King William's uniform, Stewart.'

I glanced briefly down at my red coat. 'I could wish that I still took pride in it, sir,' I told him bitterly.

'I understand.' He sighed, and beckoned Francis Farquhar to come forward. 'Lieutenant Farquhar was in the same frame of mind after his experiences in Glencoe.'

With a sudden surge of curiosity that swamped my wariness I turned to Francis exclaiming, 'So you *were* there! What happened to you?'

Francis glanced a question at Major Forbes. He frowned and said impatiently:

'Very well – you may tell him now. But we must get quickly to the main matter, so be brief, Farquhar.'

'Yes, sir,' Francis said, and turning back to me he went on rapidly, 'I was with the party Hamilton took from Ballachulish by way of Kinlochleven and over the Devil's Staircase to block the eastern end of Glencoe. I knew what our purpose was in the glen but I had no time to think about it for the blizzard forced us to fight every inch of the steep climb over the Devil's Staircase. We were six hours late in arriving in Glencoe as a result of this and Hamilton was furiously out of temper at the check to his plans. He ordered me to shoot the first person we met in the glen – a feeble old man who tried to run from our advance.'

He paused and looked away from me. Then his eyes came back to me again and very quietly he added, 'That taught me the full meaning of our orders. I refused to obey Hamilton. He ordered Gil Kennedy to shoot the old man. Gil also refused. Hamilton then shot the old man himself and had Gil and me arrested and sent south in chains to await court-martial – which we would still be doing if it had not been for Major Forbes!'

I glanced at Forbes for further enlightenment and he explained, 'I considered it my duty to take up their case in view of my own attitude to the affair.'

'I knew you had quarrelled with Hamilton at Ballachulish over the orders, sir,' I told him, and when he only nodded in reply to this I dared to ask, 'What *was* your attitude to the affair, sir?'

His face expressionless he said, 'If you are wondering why I did not rebel flatly against the orders as you junior officers did, let me remind you that the higher a soldier's rank, the greater his responsibility for intelligent action. My attitude was to do everything in my power to stop the massacre, both by appealing to the Colonel and by opposing Hamilton. When these courses failed, I marched with Hamilton in the hope of mitigating the slaughter and with the intention of gaining eye-witness evidence of his actions.'

I flushed with embarrassment at the way he had defined my unspoken challenge and disposed of it, and with a grim little smile at my confusion he added, 'My failure to stop the mass-acre made me all the more determined that Farquhar and Kennedy would not suffer for their humanity, and so I managed to obtain an order for their release on parole – to be used once I had satisfied myself of their continuing loyalty to the King.'

A sudden wild stab of hope went through me at these last words of his, but quickly I suppressed it. The Major was looking at me intently. His eyes seemed to be searching my inmost thoughts and I turned my face from him so that he could not read the expression on it.

'Ensign Stewart,' he said, 'I am authorized to offer you your parole on the same terms as Kennedy and Farquhar obtained theirs. The Army still needs officers in Flanders. It needs you, if you can assure me you are still loyal to the King and are willing to accept this condition of your parole.'

I almost had to clap my hand to my mouth to stop myself blurting out an instant acceptance of his offer, and it was only with a great effort of will that I swallowed the eager words which rose to my lips.

When I felt I could trust myself to speak again I said, 'Sir, I cannot answer you till I know where the guilt of Glencoe should lie. Glenlyon let slip to me that the Earl of Breadalbane was concerned in it, and I also suspect there were others who had a hand in the planning of it. Yet the orders for the massacre stated – *"This is by the King's special commands"*, and I cannot – I cannot—'

I stopped there and turned away from him altogether, despairing of the effort of putting the rest of my feelings into words. Forbes gripped my shoulder and swung me round to face him again.

'So,' he said, 'it is the terms of the order you carried to Glenlyon that troubles you.'

I nodded, not intending to say any more, but still could not help crying out,

'Why did the King do it, sir! How *could* he bring himself to give such an order!'

'King William gave no such order!'

Forbes fairly roared the words at me, and as I stood staring at him in astonishment he thrust his hand inside his coat and pulled out a paper.

'*This* is the order the King gave about Glencoe,' he told me, and unfolding the paper he read aloud, '*If MacIan and that tribe can well be separated from the rest it will be a proper work of justice to extirpate that set of thieves.*'

He thrust the paper at me. 'There! Read it for yourself!'

Quickly I scanned it. It was an order signed by the King and dated from London on the 16th of January of that year. The greater part of it was taken up with instructions to treat with Glengarry if he continued stubborn in holding out in his castle, and the brief reference to Glencoe came – almost like an after-thought, in the last two lines of the order.

Twice I read the order, with relief and bewilderment struggling for place in my mind, then I looked from it to Forbes and stammered:

'But – but there is no word here of putting all to the sword under seventy – no mention of planting men by stealth to rise and murder their hosts!'

'That,' said Forbes, 'is exactly what I have been trying to convey to you!'

He had himself under control again. He took the order from me and put it carefully back into his coat, then patiently he went on.

'Listen, lad, and I'll explain. The massacre was planned by Secretary of State, Stair, and by the Earl of Breadalbane – Stair because he intended to frighten the Highland Chiefs into keeping their oath of allegiance, and Breadalbane because he wanted revenge on MacIan. They needed an order signed by the King before they could move against MacIan, however, and they had to obtain this without letting the King know their true designs.

'Breadalbane set to work, therefore, to convince him that Glencoe was a sort of robbers' nest which endangered the whole peace of the Highlands, and since Breadalbane is official adviser to the Government on Highland affairs, the King naturally believed him. Stair then entered the picture with the news that MacIan had failed to take the oath in time.'

'But the Sheriff at Inveraray wrote to the Privy Council

explaining how this had happened,' I protested. 'His letter recommended that MacIan should be taken into the King's mercy.'

'That letter never reached the King,' Forbes said. 'Stair saw to that! So far as King William knew, MacIan was still in rebellion against him. It was Stair also who composed the order you have just read, and you will have noticed how carefully he worded that small, casual reference to Glencoe. "Extirpate" means "to root out", and the Macdonalds are named as the "set of thieves" that Breadalbane had described to the King. It was in the belief that he was advising the sensible course of rooting-out this dangerous nest of traitors and robbers that the King signed the order. Stair then had the authority he needed to act against MacIan.

'As to the way in which this authority was to be interpreted – the treachery of planting Glenlyon's troop among the Macdonalds, the butchery of young and old, the pincer-movement of troops to close the exits of the glen to the survivors – that had all been decided on weeks before. Lieutenant Colonel Hamilton had been chosen to command the operation, and the whole scheme of the massacre had been discussed in a secret correspondence between Stair and himself—'

'Sir!' In high excitement I interrupted Forbes. 'I know of that correspondence! Francis – Lieutenant Farquhar was told of it by Lieutenant Kennedy when Kennedy was on dispatch duty in January! I recall that we wondered why the knowledge of it was being kept from Colonel Hill.'

Grim-faced, Forbes explained, 'The Colonel was passed over in the chain of command because it was feared that he would not be ruthless enough to carry out the plan for the massacre.'

'But all the secrets are out now, Rob!' Francis put in quickly. 'There is a Jacobite spy – a fellow called Charles Leslie, who has managed to lay hands on the copies that Stair kept of all his secret correspondence with Hamilton and Breadalbane! He has been busy writing pamphlets about it and the whole story has become common knowledge since he published these.'

'Nor has Gordon, your host, been idle these past six weeks,'

Major Forbes added. 'In fact, Stewart, such a ferment of indignation over Glencoe has been raised already that now the outcry has reached London and is being echoed here. And in Edinburgh, there is growing pressure from a group of influential men for a Royal Commission to inquire into the guilt of the matter.'

He paused. 'Have I said enough to convince you that this guilt rests on others than the King – that if you continue to wear his uniform you can do so proudly?'

I nodded thankfully, quite unable to speak for the moment with the great surge of relief that was choking in my throat. Forbes gave me time to recover myself before he said:

'The offer of parole still stands, Ensign Stewart.'

'Sir,' I asked, 'Permission to shout my acceptance of the offer?'

'Permission granted, Ensign Stewart,' he told me gravely, and I opened my lungs in a long, wordless shout of relief and pure joy.

Francis and the Major watched me, grinning at the sight I made, and as my shout died away into gasping Francis asked:

'You understand that you and Gil and myself, as well as Major Forbes, will be called on to give evidence before this Commission's inquiry?'

'I do indeed,' I told him triumphantly. Then doubt struck me and I turned to Major Forbes, demanding, 'Sir, are you sure this inquiry will take place?'

'There can be no question of it,' he answered. 'The King must hold an inquiry to satisfy the Highlands that justice is being done, otherwise they will rise in revenge for the massacre. Moreover, he must vindicate himself in the matter, or he will risk losing his throne in the revival of sympathy for the Jacobites that agitators like Leslie are stirring up.'

'So we will be given a chance to clear our names, Rob,' Francis said.

'And I can help to clear the King's name also,' I reminded him. 'Remember that I saw the order that was sent to Glenlyon. I can testify how much it abused the King's authority – how far it differed from the original order signed by him.'

'There are those who have realized that already since you

escaped from Appin,' Forbes remarked a trifle maliciously. 'Hamilton is living in deadly fear of having to account for his actions, and Breadalbane has already sent an agent into Appin to try and bribe the Macdonalds into silence over his part in it. Your great-aunt set the dogs on the fellow when he came to Eilidh!'

Francis and he laughed heartily at this, but recollection of the Macdonalds sobered me. True, there was retribution in store for those responsible for their plight, but the processes of law could be long. What was to become of the Macdonalds in the meantime? I voiced this thought aloud and Forbes said reassuringly:

'They are safe enough where they are for the moment, Stewart, and Colonel Hill is taking advantage of public feeling to try and have them re-instated in Glencoe. Their allies in Clan Donald are already rallying to help them with presents of seed and livestock for their return. I think you will find that the Macdonalds, like the phoenix, will rise from the ashes again.'

'And I have news of another event that will certainly not be long delayed,' Francis said, the wide grin returning to his face. 'Elizabeth and I are to be married before we leave for Flanders!'

'*Married!*' I repeated incredulously. 'But – Great-aunt Euphemia! How did you persuade *her*?'

'There was no persuasion needed,' Francis told me, chuckling. 'When Major Forbes and I went to Eilidh to find out from her where you were hiding, we found her full of Elizabeth's lucky escape from having married into a family with the stigma of Glencoe on it. She told me I could have Elizabeth since I seemed to be the man she desired and had apparently acted like a gentleman! She also instructed me to marry her promptly, as she was tired of having such a wilful girl on her hands!'

'I think,' said Major Forbes laughing with us at this, 'that we should drink a toast to the wilful bride.'

I rushed to get the wine. We all drank a toast to Elizabeth and then filled our glasses to drink another to ourselves and to our future.

As Major Forbes took his glass from me he said, 'You may

encounter Glenlyon again, Stewart, since he is also going to Flanders, but you will not serve under him again for I am making arrangements to have you transferred to another Regiment.'

He put his glass down, nodding to Francis, and as if this had been a prearranged signal, Francis left the room. When he had gone Major Forbes told me, 'The trooper waiting outside has your sword and pistol with him, Stewart. Glenlyon brought them back to the Fort with him after the massacre so that they could be used at the formalities of your court-martial – which will not now take place, of course.'

Very awkwardly, because of the feeling that was in me, I muttered, 'I have much to thank you for, sir.'

With some bitterness he replied, 'No thanks are due to me, lad. I am only trying to see a small measure of justice brought out of this miserable affair!'

He sighed. 'I made a vain enough bid for justice when I first discovered what was intended in Glencoe and appealed to Colonel Hill to countermand the order for massacre. It was useless! I found myself talking, not to the brave, experienced soldier I had always known till then, but only to a sick old man who had learned too late that he had been passed over in the chain of command and was afraid of losing his pension rights if he tried to assert his proper authority again. And by the time I had argued all this out with him I had lost my chance for effective action.'

'I had thought better of Colonel Hill,' I said scornfully. 'I did not think he would put a paltry pension before the saving of so many lives!

'Enough, boy!' Forbes held up a hand that forbade me to say any more on these lines, and added, 'Colonel Hill has served his country honourably as a soldier for more than forty years of his life, and for the last few of these years the miserliness of the Government has compelled him to pay all the expenses of garrisoning the Fort out of his own pocket! His whole personal fortune has been drained away in this, so that now the same paltry pension is all that stands between him and starvation when he retires from the Service.'

172

Francis came in then, carrying my sword and pistol. Smiling, he gave them to me and I put them on. I was clumsy because my fingers were trembling so with excitement, but I managed to get them properly in position. When I was ready I drew myself to attention in front of Major Forbes, still finding it difficult to believe how completely his appearance had altered the outlook for me, and still marvelling that only half an hour before I had been holding him at pistol-point. Forbes inspected me gravely, then he lifted his glass again and looked at us each in turn.

'Well, gentlemen,' he said, 'you each risked your future career in the Army by your actions in Glencoe, but it was only because you were willing to sacrifice that career that you were able to save it, with honour, in the end. I wish good health and rapid promotion to both of you!'

We lifted our glasses and faced him. 'Health and promotion, gentlemen,' the Major said.

We bowed our acknowledgment of the toast.

Then Francis turned to me and raising his glass even higher he cried, 'And to that toast I add another – To Flanders!'

'Aye – to Flanders!' I shouted, and we drank both toasts together.

'Now,' said Major Forbes when the ceremony was over, 'you have your horse here, I believe, Ensign Stewart – that swift young grey you are so proud of.'

'Yes, sir.'

'Then saddle up – saddle up!' he told me briskly. ' 'Tis a long way to Flanders, my lad. We have not time to waste!'

I needed no second telling. Within minutes I had distributed the remains of my purse among my guards. I gave the head forester his share and left a message with him for my host before I rushed to the stables to bring Shadow out. Forbes marshalled his troop and gave the order to set forth and I put Shadow to the first mile of the journey south to receive our marching orders for Flanders.

Thus it happened that at last, and in spite of everything, I rode off to war as I had always dreamed of doing – with a good mount under me and the weapons my father had bequeathed to me honourably by my side. No drums beat for me as they would beat for the rest of the Regiment marching out of the Fort, and no banners flew, but I did not feel the lack of these. I had a singing in my heart that was all the music I needed, and the bright flag of honour still untarnished was banner proud enough for me.

Epilogue

I did meet Glenlyon in Flanders as Forbes had warned I might, but only on one occasion.

It was while I was riding with dispatches one night that I came late to a tavern where officers were billeted, and in the tap-room there I approached some officers grouped round a table. There was much noise of talk going on, but as I neared the table one voice rose above the rest. It was a high-pitched Highland voice slightly slurred by wine – Glenlyon's voice.

'I would do it all again, I tell you!' he was insisting. 'If I had Glencoe to do all over again I would massacre every last one of them!'

'You are only whistling in the dark, Glenlyon!' another voice cried.

In a burst of sarcastic laughter at this jeer the group of officers shifted and eddied and suddenly there was a clear space in front of me and I was looking straight to where Glenlyon was seated at the table. Our eyes met, and at the look of recognition that passed between us the others fell silent.

'Ensign Stewart!' he said thickly. Then he noticed the insignia of my rank and corrected himself, '*Lieutenant* Stewart! My little runaway Ensign has become a lieutenant!'

Mockingly he raised his cup and drank a toast to my promotion, then banging it down on the table so that the dregs spilled, he snarled at me,

'So the Enquiry is putting out a warrant for my arrest, is it! They believed your story, you miserable, sneaking, runaway rebel!'

He railed on at me and I stared at him noting his disordered hair, his haggard face and wide, feverish eyes. I made no answer to his taunts but when he fell silent at last for lack of breath I asked softly:

'What ghosts haunt you, Glenlyon? Does MacIan stand, murdered, beside your bed at night? Does his lady wander with bleeding hands through your sleep?'

Glenlyon jerked backwards like a man struck suddenly in the face, his whole body rigid with the shock of the challenge in my quiet questions. Tense, he stared at me with fearful eyes for a long moment before his body loosened and began to sag again. His mouth opened slackly. He tried to speak, and failed, and the officers around us looked coldly at him, their faces grown suddenly taut with distaste. I continued to pin his stare with my own, and remorselessly I pressed him.

'Whose face do you see in the dark, Glenlyon? Is it Inverrigan's, staring sightless at you from a-top a pile of corpses? Or is it the face of a little boy upturned in useless pleading to you as a dagger pierces his tender neck?'

A moaning sound escaped Glenlyon's slack lips. He swayed, with his eyes half-closed, and then slowly he slumped forward till his head rested on the table. For a moment longer I stood there looking at him. Then I turned and left him there with his haggard face resting in the wine-dregs, and thronging all round him, the silent avenging company of the ghosts of Glencoe.